GYPSY GRACE

A NOVEL

BY
JOAN BANNAN

Author photo by:
Bryan Batty aka Batman

Gypsy Grace Portrait by:
Sherre Bernardo

ISBN: 978-1-7333483-0-0 (hc)
ISBN: 978-1-7333483-1-7 (sc)
ISBN: 978-1-7333483-2-4 (e)
ISBN: 978-1-7333483-3-1 (audio)

Printed in the United States of America

JB Communications rev. date: September 30, 2019

Dedication

To Sandy Isganitis

Brilliant Friend and Confidant

CHAPTER ONE

Arranged Marriages

My mother gets all worked up when I call us gypsies. She says, "A true gypsy is Romani, has dark skin, and tells fortunes. We're Irish Travelers. Churchgoers. Not fortune tellers. We're not like them except we've been travelin' like them for generations."

I still call myself a gypsy but not around Mamai. I like it. It feels romantic to me, though most of our customs regarding romance are far from it. All of our marriages are arranged by our fathers. Mamai, my aunts, and cousins have always accepted it, and for the most part, our fathers did not do a horrible job of choosing. I've always had an inkling that I might be the first woman to rebel, seek freedom, and become an "outsider." Am I justifying my behavior? Maybe, but it was time for change, and when you hear my story, I think you will agree.

Generations of Travelers have believed that men were in charge; women did as they were told and nothing else. I've known for a long time that "nothing else" was not going to cut it for me. Long before I got my Liberal Arts Bachelor's Degree online, receiving accolades from teachers and peers for my creative writing papers, I was infatuated with the idea of becoming a writer. It wasn't an impossible dream. Within Travelers' social boundaries, I still imagined possibilities.

1

Reverence for men, especially those who were head of a household, was expected and enforced. My pa reigned like a king over us kids and Mamai. Especially Mamai. We're regularly reminded to keep to ourselves, which necessitated homeschooling. No community sports or, God forbid, dances or proms.

We had strict Traveler traditions, rigid family rules, and ample family chores, often enforced with extreme punishments. My heart ached each time my always-hungry, little brother Billy was sent to bed early with no dinner. My fourteen-year-old sister Danee was forced to stay in a closet all day when she was caught flirting at the roller rink with a young man, an outsider. I could tell Mamai didn't agree with Danee's punishment, but Mamai didn't do or say anything to contradict Pa. It was just not done. That was not the first time I noticed Mamai straying to the edges of sanity. While Danee was confined to the dark closet, Mamai kept forgetting what she was doing, wandering from the kitchen to the garage and then the laundry room, never completing whatever tasks she had already started. At one point, she came back empty-handed from the garage refrigerator to a kitchen filled with smoke. The smoke alarm screeched at us because she prematurely lit the fire beneath a pan and walked away. Her behavior reminded me of how she was in our family's darkest hour. It was during the years when we were still traveling.

Our brother, Johan, was born between my sisters, Uny and Danee. Pa didn't even try to hide his favoritism for his firstborn son. Johan took advantage, often ignoring Pa's direction.

At a familiar lake somewhere in Georgia, Uny, Johan, and I impatiently did our part to set up camp. We were longing to escape from the sweaty heat to the cool water. Pa finally gave us permission to go but hollered after us, "Be careful! The lake is low from the drought."

Johan laughed as he raced ahead of us to the end of the pier. He turned and grinned at us, "This is the day you will remember as the day you almost caught Captain Johan Sparrow!" He did a perfect swan dive.

Uny and I reached the end of the pier and waited for him to surface. "Maybe he's teasing us? He's probably under the pier. Hold my legs." I laid down on my stomach. Uny held me steady as I bent at the waist and hung over the edge to look beneath the wooden slats. I expected to see Johan looking up making a funny face and mocking us. Instead, he was floating face down. I stood up, jumped in and swam to him. I rolled him face up. He wasn't breathing. "Uny, run for Pa!" The water was too deep to have steady footing. I swam to the bottom and pushed off as hard as I could and then pulled Johan out from under the pier into the blazing sunshine. When it was finally shallow enough to be steady, I tried to give him some of my breath.

Even after all these years, the worst of my nightmares climax with the terror of Mamai's scream from the camp. Her wail of despair sliced through the hot afternoon and, like a razor, carved a new pattern in our lives. Johan's broken neck broke Mamai as the death of a child breaks any mother. Our grief during the next nine months was not only emotional. It was physical. Mamai lost a lot of weight and seemed to have lost her mind. I took over the homeschooling and all of Mamai's chores. Uny helped me with Danee and Billy. Pa was sullen and silent for a while, and then he turned cruel. He couldn't bring Johan back by enforcing stricter punishment, but he was obsessed with absolute obedience to his rule over us and particularly insisted that we listen to his warnings.

As firstborn and first daughter, I was overwhelmed with chores and too busy to get into much trouble. But just because I didn't speak up against my father's dictatorship, doesn't mean I didn't resent it. What's sad is, we were not the only dysfunctional family in our compound. We were surrounded by clans who were members of what I consider a cult.

Every few months, Traveler men organized a huge gathering to honor each other for accomplishments that proved their feelings of superiority. At these venues, with great bravado, they announced betrothals or business partnerships which were often intertwined. There have been questionable unions which often included a dowry offered in lieu of a payback for a shady Traveler transaction. These gatherings were the perfect setting for Traveler elders to generally brag to one another about how great they are and how much better they are than outsiders. And of course, at these gatherings, the women served.

Pa waited until I was eighteen before he and Paddy Murphy set me up to marry Paddy's oldest son, Collen. Because Collen was not a repulsive choice, I suppressed my inner rebellion and waited to marry, hoping Collen wouldn't object to my writing ambition. Mamai knew about my studies and the degree that I attained simultaneously with my high school diploma. In fact, she not only covered for me with Pa, but she also secretly paid the online tuition.

The Murphys were to settle down in our compound shortly after I turned twenty. Their huge, three-story house, a few blocks from ours, had been in the works well over a year. After the wedding, I was supposed to move into the Murphy family estate. But now, in spite of the fact that by Traveler standards I'm practically an old maid, it's not happening. Collen died a violent and senseless death.

Collen was the flagman on a paving crew, and in spite of his bright orange vest, some stupid driver of a white pickup truck blasted Collen's body into a lane of oncoming, fast-moving cars. The hooded driver sped away while everyone was too stunned to catch sight of his license plate. One witness was certain the truck had no license plate.

So a week before our planned wedding ceremony, instead of preparing myself to marry a man I hardly knew, I found myself digging through my closet to find something to wear to his funeral. I didn't really know any of the Murphys all that well, but Paddy Murphy, who most people call "Murph" and my pa, Cooey Devlin, go way back. Our families used to travel together when I was too tiny to recollect any memories of it. Like Collen, Pa and Murph worked the roads. Together, they came up with an invention that both families call "the Doohickey." The Doohickey does something for the asphalt machines that keeps them from clogging as they did pre-Doohickey. Pa and Murph share the patent and subsequent royalties that have grown exponentially. For this reason, our two families decided to stop traveling and build mansions in Texas with a whole host of other Irish Travelers who have also come into money. The Travelers pretty much own our entire neighborhood, and we have the local Catholic church basically all to ourselves.

Uny and I walked behind Mamai and Pa into the funeral mass, genuflecting before the altar and crossing ourselves. Pa led us to sit in the third pew directly behind the Murphys. It was only Pa, Mamai, Uny, and me because Pa had excused Billy since Danee was now old enough to stay at home with him. Sitting at Murph's right side was his remaining son, Zane. I noticed Zane didn't wear a suit like his pa. He wore a plain, black T-shirt and black jeans, similar to what both he and Collen wore about six months ago at their mother's funeral. Wretched cancer! Paddy's married daughters and their families entirely filled up the remaining seats in the two front pews. Little ones were squirming. Older ones were not all that settled either. They angrily competed with each other, trying to keep the younger kids quiet.

The funeral proceeded in the way that funerals do—slowly, gently, with a sense of quiet inevitability. I felt deep sympathy for them but fought with guilt for not feeling sadness on my own behalf. I despised myself for not suffering more. I had no tears, which caused me to feel even guiltier. I couldn't even muster them when Zane stood up at the gravesite to read a poem before they lowered Collen's casket into the ground.

> Another grief too soon.
>
> Our hearts vacant and aching.
>
> In bewilderment, we cry, "No!"
>
> > Did God take his hand *before* he felt the blast of pain?
> >
> > Would that God would also take our sorrow.
>
> Yet, we have God's comfort.
>
> Faith reuniting mother and son at the throne of Jesus and His love.

After the graveside service, while my parents were consoling Murph beneath the shade of the graveyard's temporary canopy, I headed across the sprawling lawn toward our SUV to escape the blazing sun. The vehicle was parked beneath a huge tree, one of the few patches of shade in the Texas-sized cemetery.

"Grace, wait up! This is for you."

When I saw the single lily in Zane's hand, tears finally flowed. "Oh, Zane. You're so thoughtful." I gasped for air and dabbed my eyes and nose with the unused, crumpled Kleenex that I'd held in my hand for the past several hours. "Your loss is so great, much greater—your brother, and yet you thought of me."

He bowed his head and gently shook it. "And you were to marry." He took my hand and pressed the thick lily stem into my palm.

I looked into his dark blue eyes.

He looked a lot like Collen but with differences. Collen's hair had been lighter. Each time I saw him, I recall the sides had been cut short, practically shaved. Zane's hair was dark, almost black. He wore it neatly trimmed at a medium length. It was wavy, not straight and spiky as his brother's had been. Long, thick lashes surrounded eyes that were slightly too large for his face.

"I loved that poem you read at the gravesite. Who wrote it?"

He blushed and bowed his head again slightly.

"No. Really? You're a poet?" I was thinking how hot this guy was, but then, it could have been because I was sweating from dripping humidity and the brilliant Texas sun.

"Shall we continue on into the shade?" I felt a tingling at my waist as he lightly touched the small of my back, directing me beneath the enormous tree. "I mostly just read other people's poems, but occasionally I also write one. I started out trying to write lyrics, but as I composed songs on my guitar, the lyrics didn't seem to fit the music." His face spread into a grin as if he'd heard something hilariously funny. "So I've only got poems and instrumentals that sing separate, unsynchronized melodies."

Yeah. It's not merely the weather. "Will you read me some of your poems?"

He blushed again. "Maybe." He smiled in a teasing way. "Hey, I've got my truck here. Would you like to ride with me to the reception? It's got mighty air conditioning, enough for a whole SUV, but it's only a double-benched crew cab."

"Sure. Mighty air conditioning sounds mighty good right now." I glanced toward the small group lingering by the grave. "I'll text Uny to tell my parents."

CHAPTER TWO

Grace and Zane

In fairness to my pa, he may not have been aware of how much time Zane and I spent together over the next six months. Since Zane was only twenty-four, we were closer in age than Collen and I had been, and we shared other common interests besides his poetry. One was running. Zane worked as an auto mechanic, so three days a week after he had showered off the day's grease, we would meet up at the park near our homes as the sun started to fade. We'd do a few stretches and then step together in a steady rhythm along the community path that ran between our park and the elementary school two miles away. On our return, Zane would buy two bottles of cold water at the convenience store across from the park before we settled at a shady picnic table to cool down and chat.

"So Zane, what do you think about our fanatical traditions?"

He grinned at me. "Well, I can tell how you feel about them, so let me carefully choose and consider the words for my answer."

"I suppose my adjective betrayed me."

"What bothers you the most?"

"I think it's the hatred of outsiders. It's as if our people assume we are smarter or nobler than others, but the worst part is the way we use it as an excuse to con and swindle people."

"Yeah. I haven't noticed it with my pa or yours, maybe it's because long ago they boosted their income with the Doohickey, but when we were on the road, many of the men in the families we traveled with, often swindled each other."

"Really?"

"Yeah. I saw them steal jobs from each other, sometimes usurping deals by lying to the people who were willing to hire. I'm relieved our families no longer scrabble and roam."

"How did you learn to be a mechanic?"

"My pa was always good with motors and such. I hung out, observed, and learned. The more proficient and experienced I became, the more I enjoyed it. He encouraged my interest and sent me to an expensive trade school. 'It's practical,' he advised me. 'Your poems and music most likely won't keep food on your table, or even buy you a table for that matter.'"

"Do you still like being a mechanic, now that you do it as a job day after day?"

"Actually, I do. I like working with my hands and challenging my brain. I specialize in imported cars. The computerized stuff is the most fun of all. The problems our clients bring to us are entirely different than it was when I was at school. The instructors told us, 'This is how this works. This is what that is for. Here trouble-shoot this or rebuild that,' but a lot of the work that rolls into our shop is mysterious. No instructions or clues included. A woman drove in a few days ago, and it was all I could do to keep from laughing in her face as she tried to recreate the noises her car had been making. She screeched a few bars and then made some other bumpity-bump thump sounds, like this," he simulated her sounds. "She thought it would help explain what was wrong."

A woodpecker flew to the tree that shaded us and knocked on the tree trunk as if mimicking the sounds Zane had just made. I looked up at the bird's bright red head hammering for bugs. "Did you figure it out?"

"Yup, and that always feels good. More than that, this job allows me to be me."

"And who is that, Zane?" I raised my eyebrow in inquiry.

"I like to be alone with nature, like my mentor, Ward. I'm gradually buying the shop from him. He's trying to teach me everything he knows before he retires. Our leased garage is in a remarkable, wooded area. Import Automotive is the last unit in a strip mall that ends near an open field, largely sheltered with big trees and surrounded on two sides by a curving creek. We leave the bay doors open. Birdsong fills our early mornings. On our side of the creek, a bull and a steer graze. It's a curious thing. They seem to be friends. Their owner brings them food to supplement grazing and fills their drinking trough from a tank hauled in the back of her pickup. She's got the trough positioned strategically in the afternoon shade but not under the tree that shades it."

"Good call or it would be filled with bird poop."

"Right? I swear, when they see her, those two act more like dogs than a bull and a steer. They nudge her for head rubs. A chain link fence separates a grove of trees where busy birds congregate to entertain the bull, the steer, and me. Occasionally, a family of deer wanders through, eating the tender leaves of the young saplings. An expanse of land across the creek hosts a horse ranch." Zane's deep blue eyes seemed to see beyond me, beyond the park, and far away. "So while I'm working, it's quiet."

"Except for the birds."

"Right. Noisy birds but what a splendid noise. What about you, Grace? How are you doing now that you are no longer my brother's fiancé?"

My cheeks felt hot. "Well, since you asked, even when I *was* Collen's fiancé, I had a dream to be a writer. I was hoping he wouldn't mind."

"He wouldn't have minded. He's like me, I mean *was* like me." Emotion clouded his eyes. "We often chatted about what a waste of womankind our traditions fostered. Have you ever met my cousin, Liam?"

"Sort of. He was at the funeral, right? Tall, black wavy hair, with a pasty white, almost blue complexion?"

"Right. That's the one. Did you notice his wife, Megan?"

"Not really. I mostly talked to you, remember?"

One side of his mouth lifted to a smile. "Yeah. Well anyway, she's remarkably intelligent. He has a sporting goods business that would totally fail without her. Collen and I both used to remark that he may not be the sharpest tool in the toolbox, but he certainly was smart to marry her. And he knows it. He appreciates her and adores her in every way. She loves him to death for it. Thanks to their successful marriage and comradery, Collen and I would fantasize about connecting with intelligent, ambitious women ourselves."

"And if you found such women, you'd have to plead with your pa to make arrangements. It's so thorny to navigate our customs."

"So what kind of writing do you want to do?"

12

"I love stories. I read novels, probably about three per month, but I like real stories too. I wouldn't mind being a journalist who seeks out interesting people who should have their stories told. I didn't think the latter was possible though since it would take me out of the home where the Travelers think I belong. For several years now, I've been devouring instruction on how to write fiction."

"Seems like you already know a lot about fiction if you read three novels a month!"

"Maybe, but I feel inadequate. It's similar to loving classical music, which I do by the way. Listening to symphonies doesn't equip me to write one."

"I think you are destined to be a great writer, Grace. Your work and creativity will lift its wings on an updraft of wind created by your faithfulness to keep learning. Nothing you write will be laced with mediocrity because nothing mediocre defines you, only excellence, ambition, and purpose."

I pondered how Zane didn't need a pen to create poetic words that sounded grand or impressive.

After months of meeting up to run, one evening at the picnic table, I invited Zane to come to the house after dinner the next evening. After that, he habitually stopped by every Tuesday and Thursday and never came empty-handed. There was always a flower or flowers. Sometimes it was a single florist's flower. Often, he merely brought a few buttercups or other wildflowers that he sought out on the way.

The first time we settled at our kitchen table with the lemonade Mamai had put out for us, Zane didn't see the silly grin on Uny's face when she poked her head through the kitchen doorway briefly and then disappeared. I asked him, "Are you doing okay? I bet you really miss Collen, right?"

"Yes, time helps and this," he pointed at me and then himself. "Our friendship is a balm to my soul. I'm doing infinitely better than I was when we lost Mamai. I went through a dark time. I was angry and mean to my family. What's worse is, I knew it. It was as if I couldn't control myself, like I was a marionette with strings that bound me to anger and discontent, followed by embarrassment and feelings of guilt. I was a slave to negativity, wallowing in self-centered pity."

"You felt guilty for the way you grieved for your mamai?"

"Yes. A touch of insanity, huh?"

"Yeah, I mean no. Guilt seems to be my middle name lately. I totally relate."

"When we lost Mamai, I felt like the grief was mine alone, but I wasn't even her only child." He nervously fidgeted, twitching at one sleeve of his T-shirt and then the other. He took a breath. "There were my sisters and Collen but so many others. And of course, Pa, who may never be the same. So many people miss Mamai's kindness and her generosity. As much as I struggled trying to make it so, it wasn't all about me. I wanted to be kind to all of them, but I wasn't. I didn't want to be mean and selfish, but I was. It tries to creep up on me again every now and then." He paused and searched my face. "Want to know a secret? I've learned something that shuts the guilt down."

"Hey wait! We're Catholics, aren't we supposed to feel guilty and make others feel the same?"

He chuckled. "I've heard that joke before."

"I know. I couldn't let it pass. So what's your secret?"

"Each time guilt rears its negative, discouraging head, I remind myself to forgive myself."

"That's it?"

"Yes. Have you tried it?"

"Can't say I have."

"Oh gosh, Grace, I know this secret sounds so simple, but it's carried on the wings of faith in the One who loved me enough to forgive me first." Zane's eyes opened wider, he leaned forward, and his words came faster. "His forgiveness set me free to forgive myself but comes with promises and power so much greater than that. It's like the secret to life. Abundant life. I had to die to my selfishness. But it wasn't simple. I had to take that first step of surrender for everything, not just forgiveness. You know, 'deny myself and take up my cross daily?'"

"I'm not sure I do know. Just because I've heard it doesn't mean I know it and just because I know it, doesn't mean I do it." I paused to ponder the enormity of the simplicity of his secret. "I've never thought about that verse meaning that I need to die to selfishness daily. I sort of thought of it in a ubiquitous suffering way, like maybe there would be daily sacrifices for taking my faith seriously."

"I know. Me too. Suffering awakened the need in me to analyze the struggle of who I wanted to be and who I didn't want to be. I was powerless to change on my own. And you know what? It's more than just daily. It's throughout each day, moment by moment. Sometimes I feel upset about something and I ask myself, 'would a dead man feel that?' Then I answer myself, 'Nope. Seems I've fallen out of grace and need to surrender to the cross yet again.'"

"You certainly have philosophical, theological discussions with yourself."

"Yes. I suppose I do, the same people I invited to my pity party, me, myself, and I. But it's working for me, that continual surrender throughout each day. Since Collen died, I'm still lured to the precipice that drops into self-pity. If I did take that leap, everyone around me would probably still be comforting and understanding, which only intensifies the temptation to be self-centered. I'd say all of this is impossible, but it's still not about me. I have faith in God, Who says I can't live out His plan for my life without Him. When I die to myself and put my trust in Him, He makes all things possible, even continually forgiving myself. Shameful memories still surface, but I meet them with prevailing confidence that replaces the agony of regret with an unexplainable peace."

CHAPTER THREE

Wait! What? Really?

Uny, who had recently reached the illusionary, passionate age of eighteen, was convinced a new marriage arrangement was in the works. She was far more impatient for possible betrothal news than I was. When Murph was there, she combined her talent of avoiding chores with an intense interest in any quiet tasks within earshot of Pa's den. From the top of the stairs, I spotted her next to the massive bureau on the opposite side of the den's wall. When she saw me, she carefully set down one of Mamai's display teacups, put one finger in front of her lips, and violently motioned her dust rag, entreating me to come down.

When I reached her side, Uny whispered, "Paddy's in there, and they're talking about you."

We heard Pa say, "It's time, Murph."

"Yeah. I suppose it is."

"You've been down a long time. Too long. You're not on the road anymore, and you have that big house to take care of. You need a woman's touch."

We took each other's hands and grinned at each other. Uny shook from giggling silently and whispered, "See! He's going to betroth you to Zane."

I felt heat rise in my neck. I brought a shooshing finger to my lips.

"I dunno Cooey. It don't seem right."

Pa said, "Relatives after all, as we planned. This match is even more likely to give us some 'insurable interests' than the one between Collen and Grace would have."

I pondered the question, *how would a match with Zane be any more advantageous than one with Collen?*

There was a moment of silence before Pa spoke again. "It still doesn't seem right that Crosby had a policy on Collen, because it was such a long time ago that you made him godfather. Who'd a thought he'd turn so nasty toward us? I'm surprised he didn't come to Collen's funeral. Humph. I'm sure he didn't neglect to take his payout for Collen's policy though. Thanks to his policy on Aislyn, he's sittin' by the ocean in California, too preoccupied to honor the passing of his godson. It's time we seriously get on the insurance policy bandwagon like most the folks around here that started this compound."

Murph didn't answer Pa immediately as if he was thinking or maybe he drank some tea. "Your Grace is so young, and I don't want no more kids."

Uny and I both inhaled a small gasp.

"What was that?"

"Probably just the sprinklers turning on out front. She'll likely be okay with not having kids. She's different, my Grace. She always has her head in the clouds or in a book. She's into finding causes. At the dinner table, she spends more time talking about how she can save the world than she does eating. One foster child, one hungry homeless person, or one puppy at a time. It can be your turn to tame her lofty ideas and imagination. She likes kids and anyone else who needs nurturing, like that dumb squirrel she saved from

Brutus, but I think she's had enough taking care of kids by helping her mamai with our other three. It'll be fine, Murph, you need a good wife, and she's a good girl."

The heavy thumping of my heart was so loud I was afraid Pa would hear it. My abdomen clenched involuntarily; my face was hot; my eyes brimmed with tears. I squeezed Uny's hands and she shook her head as I was shaking mine, *no, no, no*. I felt a strong clamp on my arm. Mamai had a grip on Uny also. She yanked us away from the den's doorway, around the corner, down the hallway, and into the laundry room.

CHAPTER FOUR

A Mother's Heart

"You were eavesdropping on Paddy and your father." Mamai's face was darkened. I couldn't discern if it was disappointment or anger or perhaps both.

Uny spoke with a defiant tone, "Dad is arranging for Grace to marry Paddy Murphy, not Zane!"

This time I recognized the look of worry that crossed Mamai's face. She jerked her head into the hallway, glanced nervously toward the den, and then as if she were saying it to herself, "Marry Paddy Murphy? Are you sure?"

I wiped my tears with my hand. "Yes. We heard him say that exactly."

Mamai embraced me, "I'm so sorry, Gracie. This clan is so …" I felt myself shaking and sobbed silently in Mamai's arms. Mamai was also trembling.

Uny spoke in her typical hurried manner, "I thought they'd be arranging Zane and Grace."

Mamai nodded. "Me too."

"What is he? Like a hundred?" Uny retorted.

Mamai's worried look lifted, and she smiled for the first time since she had wrenched us into the laundry room. No, he's only a couple of years older than your pa, but still, I wonder why. I know they planned on connecting the families so—"

"Life insurance, right?" Uny interrupted, "They want to come up with something called 'insured interest,' like the other Traveler's families who settled here who got huge money when people died. They were talking about that too."

"Yes. They do. It's 'insurable interest.' Cousin Shelta's husband, Hogan Crosby, just collected an insurance payout for Collen Murphy. I heard he also got a huge payout when his wife, Aislyn, died."

I sensed there was more. "What Mamai? What's going on? You look like you just burned dinner."

"Oh, I suppose it doesn't matter now that Aislyn's gone. I kept her secret for over twenty years."

"Secret?" asked Uny.

"Yes." Mamai looked intently toward the hall. "Let's get out of this laundry room. I know; let's go for a walk. I'll run upstairs and put on my tennis shoes." She pointed at our feet. "Your shoes are fine. Meet me out front."

Our feet thumped in unison along the sidewalk on the opposite side of our street. The park where Zane and I met up to run came into view. We passed the last house on that side of the street and stepped into pockets of shade offered by ancient trees.

"So? The secret?"

Mamai smiled at Uny. "My most impatient child."

Uny nodded in agreement, likely considering Mamai's assessment a compliment. "Um yeah. So out with it. What secret haunts the Hogan Crosby clan? Gosh, isn't he the one with fifty kids?"

I deliberately bumped arms with Uny. "You're so silly. Always hyperbole. He only had eleven by Aislyn, and now he has a boy with Cousin Shelta, right Mamai?"

21

"Well actually. There are two secrets. The first one is that he and Aislyn had another child, but he doesn't know about it."

"Really! How could that happen?"

"We were with them, traveling in California. Aislyn was pregnant with baby number twelve. Crosby and the other men were away for a few days when the baby came. They'd landed work a few towns away, clearing out some burned trees left over from a forest fire. Aislyn met a nice lady at the corner fruit stand. Her husband, a carpenter, had given Crosby some work the week before. The lady showered Aislyn with gifts of food. She made a big deal about how lucky she was to have so many children." Mamai scoffed. "And Aislyn only had about six with her at the fruit stand. The lady told Aislyn she didn't have any kids, and now she never would be able to."

Uny's tone rose to a high pitch with her question, "And she gave the lady her baby?"

"Yep. The midwife and all of us traveling with her covered her lie. She told Crosby the baby never took a breath. Pretended that she took him to the nearest Catholic church to have him blessed and buried."

"No way!"

"Yes way, Uny. We didn't want Crosby to get angry with Aislyn. We'd seen bouts of his temper."

I retorted accusingly, "And yet Aunt Nutta let your cousin, Shelta, marry him?"

"Well, that would be the other secret—a deal between Uncle Lundy and Crosby. You may remember that Shelta wasn't the most attractive teenager. Had a hard time with embarrassing acne, and she found comfort in eating. She was twenty-four and still traveling with her family when she married Crosby, who was nearly fifty. He didn't care that she was pushing two hundred fifty pounds and—" Mamai paused.

"And what?"

"Pregnant."

'Not by Crosby?"

"No. Not by Crosby. But, he wanted another wife and didn't mind another kid. Besides marrying Shelta opened up a whole new batch of family members on whom he could prove those insurable interests, including the baby."

"Aren't some of his older kids about the same age as Cousin Shelta?"

"Yes. One set of the twins and two of the others are younger than Shelta."

"What's with us gypsies?"

Mamai stopped suddenly in one of the patches of shade. "We're not gypsies, Uny! We're not even Travelers anymore now that we're not travelin'."

Uny's voice caught and her eyes brimmed with tears. "But everyone calls us that. When I'm in stores, I know that they know; I can hear them in the next aisle. They make snide remarks about homeschooling and other stuff."

Mamai slowed her walking to give Uny a sideways hug. "I'm sorry, Uny. Yes. People are filled with contempt and resentment for others. For some reason, it's hard for them to accept people who are not like them. Not only those folks in the grocery store. All folks. Even our folks, in fact, especially our folks. They are sometimes so cruel." She shook her head slowly.

I nodded affirmatively, "When we get to Heaven, every-one will love everybody. It will be so nice to know that everybody we meet will love us. "

"Indeed, Grace, that *will* be wonderful."

Quickly recovering from her emotional interlude, Uny broke away and picked up her pace. We followed. "What does it matter what they call us anyway? And actually, they're right about us being the ones who are weird. This is just rotten and so weird that Pa would make Grace marry that old dude. You know she's in love with Zane, right?"

Was I in love with Zane or was this a romantic notion from the excessively romantic Uny?

Mamai stopped walking and turned to face me.

I turned my palms up and shrugged my shoulders think-ing, *I dunno*, but I realized right away that Mamai may have misinterpreted my body language. She may have thought I was confirming that Uny was right.

The three of us stood there momentarily until Mamai finally broke the silence, "We're almost to the picnic tables. Let's go sit there." She pointed toward the shaded table she had in mind. She had no idea she seated us at "Zane's and my table." "So Grace, is this true? Are you in love with Zane?"

"I don't know. Maybe. How can I know what love is? I do like him a lot and I really like the idea of, well, if I married him I would only be a few blocks from you." I nodded at Uny so she'd know I didn't mean only Mamai. "I was willing to go along with our cultic customs when I thought I'd marry Collen, but marry Murph? I think our customs suck. Marrying Murph seems really, really gross. And—"

Uny interrupted, "It *is* gross! Can't we do something Mamai? Can't we say, 'no'?"

Mamai patted Uny's hand and smiled. "We? My little crusader standing up for your sister."

"I'm not little. I'm eighteen! It's time we women stood up to this craziness for all of us. And I'm next, right? It's amazing that Pa hasn't already promised me to some old geezer. In fact, if he paid any attention at all to what was going on, and would have found it in his heart to promise Grace to Zane, he'd probably be arranging to give *me* to Murph!"

Mamai looked flustered. "You're probably right."

I felt the blood leave my face. "Yeah, she's right. Let me think for a minute." I took a breath and reached for Mamai's hand. "Okay. Here goes. Mamai, I don't know if I love Zane, but I like him a lot and I'm very attracted to him. I'm leaving."

Mamai looked like she had turned to stone. Her hand beneath mine was limp.

"I can't marry the father of the man I may be in love with. Can you imagine Zane and me living in that house with me married to his pa? I have to leave."

I felt Mamai's hand tense up. I saw tears rising in her eyes. She started to tremble. "But—"

"Oh, Mamai! I don't want to leave you. For that matter, I don't even want to leave Pa, but I'm going to leave. I don't know where I'm going, how I'm going to get there, or how I'm going to support myself, but I'll figure it out. I'm leaving before Pa makes me marry Murph." I slid closer to her, wrapped my arm around her, and pulled her close as she trembled and cried. I looked across at a stunned Uny. I could never remember a time when she had been speechless.

Mamai straightened up. "I'm sorry." She pulled a tissue from a small packet of Kleenex she'd retrieved from her pocket and wiped her face. She held up the packet. "I knew when I went to change my shoes, we'd need these." Her hand was trembling. "This nonsense needs to stop. I'm going to send you away to Cousin Shelta."

I felt my eyes go wide. *Mamai was going to help me?* "But, won't Shelta's husband, Crosby, rat us out?"

"Hogan Crosby hates your father and Paddy Murphy. He hasn't spoken to them in years, except to complete and sign insurance alliances. I thought since he was Collen's godfather that he'd show up for Collen's funeral, but apparently, his hatred of your Pa and Murph is bigger than his godfather promises. There's been a silent war between the three of them since they patented the Doohickey. Crosby thought he should've been included in the patent because he was working alongside them when they invented it."

"So, won't he hate me too?"

"No. I'm guessing he'll consider it worthy revenge if he harbors you and keeps you away from your father. Besides…"

"Besides?" I asked.

"Crosby loves women. When we traveled with him, all of us women were captivated by his charms." She grinned. "He never cheated on Aislyn. It wasn't like that, but he was, well, he'd hang out with us sometimes instead of the men if he could. He'd volunteer to help us with chores that the other men considered women's work. Even nasty chores."

"Hey wait! What about me? If you send Grace away—"

"I know," Mamai said. "You'll both have to go." She pulled out another tissue, and this time she did not apologize for her tears.

Mamai's words sunk into me with accountable weight. Uny too. My flight to freedom would bear considerable consequences. A tornado of emotion, terrible and wild, began to swirl deep within me. We would be leaving so much love behind, Mamai, whose psyche has been so fragile,

Pa, Danee, Billy, and Zane. I had a twinge of unexplained panic about how our escape might influence Uny's life. My thoughts and fears tangled up in my gut, winding back on themselves, causing a snarled-up feeling, something like heartburn. And then, of course, there were multi-layered feelings of guilt, over which I longed to experience the victory Zane tried to explain to me.

CHAPTER FIVE

Anita Fox Devlin

Trying to suppress her self-reproach and keep her betrayal of Cooey on the back burner of her brain, Anita focused on her plans to liberate Grace and Uny from the Travelers' heartless, archaic traditions. She stretched her arm around to the back of the washing machine and tugged free a Ziplock bag. She slipped the cash, two-thousand, five-hundred, twenty dollars, into her handbag. Her first stop: the post office. She paid the annual fee in advance for a post office box so the statement to her new bank account wouldn't come to the house. She chose their family bank for her secret checking account. No one could report to Cooey that she'd be seen where she wasn't expected to be. He was so controlling; she knew he probably knew exactly where she was by tracking her phone as he did the girls' phones. As the bank promised, Anita received the ATM/debit card in a few days. As soon as it arrived, she used her cell phone to authorize the bank card and headed to the library. Cooey was too much of a homebody and denbody for her to risk using the laptop in his study. She used a library computer to check schedules and buy bus tickets. She drove to Target and purchased two prepaid cell phones, one for her and one for the girls.

"I called Shelta. She'll be expecting you on Friday. She's excited to have you come. They own a little motel right on the ocean. She will let you stay in one of the motel rooms most of the time, but if they get totally booked, you'll move in with them and sleep on couches until the busy time passes."

"Wow! The Pacific Ocean. California. This will be an adventure!"

She found a smile for the effervescent Uny sitting across the same picnic table she'd chosen previously. A flock of finches was noisily making themselves known in the tree that shielded them from the westerly sun. Anita fought the pain in her gut. She hadn't felt well since she started to process the upcoming loss of her two oldest daughters. She was acutely aware of her disgraceful betrayal of her husband's trust and her defiance of everything Cooey Devlin lived for. She felt nauseated. Her actions would inevitably wound him. Other than anger, he rarely showed deep feelings for his family. It was as if he feared all other emotions. His identity was wrapped up in what he considered benevolent control of each of them. Whether he admitted it to himself or anyone else, he would be deeply hurt.

"Well, Uny, you keep thinking that. Your enthusiasm for the outrageous should motivate the practical, responsible Grace to get through the first part of this. And then, when reality sets in, she'll be the one to protect you, as always." She patted Grace's hand. "You'll both need to work for Shelta and Crosby, you know."

"For free?"

"I'm not sure, Uny. It may be to pay for your room and board, or they might also compensate you. We need to be grateful for whatever, right?"

"Right."

"Grace, as soon as you can manage it, I want you to open a checking account at a local bank." Anita's felt her hand trembling as she passed Grace an envelope. "Here's some starter cash." As soon as you have the account and routing numbers, text them to me. "You've got thirty-seven hours of buses ahead of you, including four transfers, and I counted at least sixteen stops." She pulled two cell phones from her bag and unsuccessfully tried to control the hand that slid the pink one to Grace.

"Mamai, are you okay?" Grace picked up her mother's hand instead of the phone.

Anita felt the presence of potential tears somewhere behind her eyes, but she didn't allow them to break free. She squeezed Grace's hand and then drew her own hand back to tap her tiny black phone. "I've loaded the number to this one into yours. You can call me any time and not worry that your pa will hear it. Just leave a message. It will be always turned off in its hiding place. I've also loaded Shelta's cell number and the phone number and address of Seal Harbor Inn in Pacific Grove. Your last bus will land you in Monterey. You'll need to find a transit bus to take you the last leg of the trip. I didn't try to buy transit tickets ahead of time, though it could probably be done. You'll figure it out." She handed a smaller envelope to Grace. "Here are your Greyhound tickets and enough cash to cover the transit bus from here to Austin, the transit bus at the end of the line, and your food along the way. You'll mostly be on Greyhound buses, but the other buses will probably also have onboard bathrooms, Wi-Fi, and power outlets. You can take your iPads. Leave your cell phones here though. Your pa tracks both of you with a GPS app."

Grace looked up from studying the pink phone in her palm. "Oh, Mamai. I'm so going to miss you!"

The tears gained ground, but Anita took a deep breath. "We need to be brave." She tilted her head back and sniffed. "Your Greyhound leaves Austin at 3:05 AM. Tonight you'll need to have everything ready so you can slip out to catch the 2:00 AM Gorman Village transit from the corner." She pointed to the far side of the park that bordered on Romp Street.

"They run that early?"

"Actually they run that late. The bars stop serving at two in the morning. Soon after, the last transit bus runs for the night. They start up a few hours later. I wish I could drive you and see you off or take you to Austin, but I can't think of anything that wouldn't make your pa suspicious. Until then, for the rest of today and through the evening, we need to go through our day as if nothing has changed. Tonight, your last dinner at home," she wiped under her eyes and sniffed, "needs to be a normal dinner, though I'm fixing the meatloaf that you both love."

CHAPTER SIX

Goodbye to Zane

Apprehension and sadness saturated my thoughts. I yearned to tell Zane that Uny and I were leaving. To say goodbye without letting him know that we may be gone forever would be callous. My heart was aching, not only because of Zane. I was successfully sabotaging today's happiness with tomorrow's sorrow. My little sister and brother would no longer know day to day how much I loved them. I could hardly process how much I was going to miss Mamai. And, in spite of his repulsive plan to give me in marriage to Murph, I was sorry to leave Pa and felt overwhelmed with guilt for the profound hurt I was about to inflict on him. Could I trust Zane to keep our secret? Mamai told us to act normally. Normally. As if the entire world wasn't transforming in the next twenty-four hours. I needed to make some lame excuse and lie to Zane or I needed to trust him. I knew he'd stop by after dinner with at least one flower in hand.

"Hi." Zane blushed before he handed me a red rose for the first time. "Wow, a dress! A pretty white dress. No jeans. Is this a special occasion?" He clutched a single sheet of typed paper in his other hand.

"Um, well thank you. I'm doing all my other laundry and I spotted this in my closet so I thought, 'Why not wear something pretty at dinner?'" I continued my unnecessary explanations. "It's also a cool choice for a day like this. Come in, come in out of the heat." A huge fly zoomed through before I could close the door behind Zane. "Rats! I hate those filthy bugs. Oh well, maybe it will go into the kitchen. We're in here this evening." I motioned to the somewhat private, corner of our massive living room. "Mamai made us some fresh lemonade." I glanced curiously at the paper.

Zane pulled the paper close to his chest. "Not yet." He placed it face down on the coffee table, out of my reach.

I handed him a glass of lemonade and poured one for myself. I dreaded wasting our time with small talk. Being alone would inevitably be short-lived in this household of six. In fact, as if on cue, Pa came out of his den, spotted us, and took a single step toward us onto the living room carpet.

"Hey, Zane. How are you, son? I was just going out with your pa to the driving range. I thought you might be coming along, but I guess not."

Zane rose from his seat saying, "Hi Mr. D, yes, I'm good. Thanks for inquiring. No. Not headed anywhere but here tonight. Pretty tired from a long day's work. There was a mystery fuel leak on a Mercedes today that 'bout drove me to distraction, but I finally figured it out and fixed it." He took one hand in the other and held them up in victory, like the winner of a prize fight.

Pa and I both chuckled.

"It felt good, but it tuckered me out."

I was watching Pa's face as he nervously surveyed our intimate lemonade rendezvous. He seemed troubled. Did it dawn on him at this very moment that hard-working, silly Zane was obviously courting me? Was he reconsidering the cruelty of his plans for me? "Well, er," Pa waved his hand in a kingly command, "please son, sit down and relax. I'll be on my way."

As soon as I heard the inner garage door close behind Pa, I turned to Zane and asked, "Can I trust you to keep a secret?"

He searched my face and looked a little hurt. "Of course." He laid his hand upon his heart. "What is it? You seem jumpy."

"I'm sorry. Yeah, I am crazy jumpy. I'm leaving. I'm taking Uny with me. Mamai is helping, but Pa doesn't know."

The blood drained from Zane's face. "Away? Forever? Why? When?"

"Tomorrow. Yeah, it's probably forever. Um, we're rebelling at the stupid traditions. My pa wants me to marry your pa."

"No, no. That's not right, especially since—"

"I know, right?" I pulled out the pink cell phone. "Here is my secret number. When you save it into your phone, don't put my name in with it in case anyone sees it." I stopped talking and tapped the phone. "Please give me your number again." I typed it in as he gave it to me. I wished I had engaged my brain instead of trusting the phone to memorize his number. I wanted my entire message to be the heart emoji, but the phone Mamai gave me was not a smartphone. It wouldn't have mattered. His flip phone was not a smartphone either, so I just typed <3.

His phone dinged. He looked down and grinned. With a yearning tone, he asked, "A great, tortuous distance? Too physically far away to see you in person," he reached out and took my hand, "and touch you?"

"Yes. Really far. Northern California. Near Monterey. I guess—maybe someday you could come to visit. We're leaving tonight; well, it's technically early tomorrow morning. Please stop by, expecting to see me, Thursday evening as you always do or Mamai will know I told you. Besides that, Pa may think you were in on it."

He handed me the paper which read,

I could not wait though words and courage fail me

Boldness through virtuosity

Proclaiming ardor

Daring to risk rejection of both.

I dared to hope that words are yet unsaid.

Mutual devotion?

Adoration?

Passion?

Reciprocated or solo in this fascination?

My voice cracked, "I don't know what to say." I swallowed hard to fight the rising tears.

When I walked him to the front door, I asked, "Why are you staring at me?"

"I'm memorizing your face, your eyes, your hair, and your lips." He lifted my chin with his hand. "May I?"

I smiled. "I wish you would."

The first kiss in my life was a kiss goodbye.

CHAPTER SEVEN

Texas to California

Before our bus trip from Texas to California, I suspected that Uny might be the friendliest, most outgoing person I may ever know. Afterward, I was entirely sure that she was. Uny didn't consider herself rebellious to disregard Mamai's warnings not to talk to strangers. In Uny's world, everyone was a potential, fascinating friend. She spent much of our thirty-seven hours coaxing stories out of each of the new friends who were destined to sit in our row in the "Uny hot seat" a few feet across the aisle from her. When I was not interacting with them, I would write about them in my notebook or take notes in my iPad. However, Uny was relatively quiet during the first hour and a half from Austin to San Antonio, but then it was only four AM. During the first two-hour, ten-minute layover, over breakfast burritos and coffee she suggested, "Let's play a game."

"What game?"

"I dunno, but we've got a long way to go. It'll make it seem shorter, and it'll be more fun."

I pondered this for a few minutes and took a sip of coffee. "I know! Let's find as many palindromes as we can along the way. Remember when Mom had us make up sentences like, 'Was it a bat I saw?' Or 'was it a cat I saw?' and things like that?"

"You called her Mom. You never call her Mom; why are you grinning?"

"Mom is a palindrome."

"Oh! Good one. Yeah. This is a perfect time to start this game as we are sitting near the San Antonio 'Civic' Center." She used air quotes to surround the word civic.

"Yes! You catch on fast. Remember, this one? It's perfect for us today, 'Are we not drawn onward to new era?'"

"Wow!"

"Excellent! Hey, okay, let's go. That's our bus that just rolled up." I waved my hand in front of my nose. "We've got a lot of disgusting diesel exhaust ahead."

"Indeed, smellems."

"Yeah, that's a palindrome, but it's not a word. Come on. Let's load our bags. Give me your claim check. I'll put them together here in the outside pocket of my backpack. The ticket agent told me we need to show them to get our bags off the bus at each transfer, but we don't have to get new ones to check them onto each new bus."

"Wasn't the ticket agent named Eve?"

"No, I mean I don't remember, Uny? Why?"

She grinned mischievously, "Eve. Palindrome. Maybe Bob will be our driver."

"I like it. I think there's one about nodding too. I'll have to work on that one. See if I can remember it on the way. Let's board early. I'm tired. Do you mind if I take a window seat? I'll probably be able to nap all the way to—" I looked down at our itinerary in my hand, "Texas Junction."

"Sure. I like the aisle so I can—"

She and I said simultaneously, "Talk to people."

I was able to nap on and off for most of the next few hours. Uny slept for a while too, but at sunrise when I returned from the bathroom and squirmed in front of Uny to return to my seat, she was pulling information from a sleepy-eyed woman across the aisle who had recently woken. The woman looked like she was only in her mid-thirties or so but had had a hard life. Her hair was long and brown, laced heavily with frizzy grays. It was pulled up into a ponytail revealing a colorful butterfly tattoo on the back of her neck. She was wearing jeans that seemed too large, as if she'd lost a considerable amount of weight since the last time she'd worn them. Both her tank top and her denim shirt, worn open as a jacket, were also too roomy for her small frame.

She answered Uny's questions with a warm smile behind her eyes. "Yeah. I'm not going far, just to El Paso. Got a friend there. At least I hope he's still my friend." She bobbed her head as if trying to assure herself with little nods of yeses.

"He doesn't know you're coming?"

"He said I could come as soon as I got out of jail, but he don't know that I'm out yet. I don't have a phone, nor his number, just the address where he was supposebly going. Spent the night in a motel so gross it was way worse than the county jail. This is the first bus out."

Uny's arm, resting next to mine, tightened when the woman mentioned jail, but though her posture stayed tense, it didn't alter my sweet sister's demeanor toward the woman. At first, I thought the mention of being incarcerated might put Uny at a loss for words, but it would take more than that. "My name is Uny. What's yours?"

"Anna. Anna Mae." She blurted out as if she'd waited a long time to put into words, "I didn't mean to kill that man."

Uny and I both took a sharp breath and stared at Anna.

She began her story defensively, as if she had rehearsed it, or as if it had involuntarily run repeatedly run through her brain, waiting for an opportunity to be told. "I was drivin'

Elliot's car 'cause I was relatively soberer than he was. This guy stepped right out in front of the car. He was drunk too. How funny is that? He never seen me. I never seen him, but I felt him and I stopped. They told me his name was Zeke Hardie and he didn't have a new family, just the old one he was born into. They said his mama cried for him, but she's warned him that drinkin' would kill him. I cried for him too, pretty much every night since. Anyway, they gave me three years in the county jail for vehicular manslaughter. Didn't even go to court. I just said 'okay' when they made the offer. Elliot said he was movin' to El Paso for a job, and I could find him there at his mother's when I got out." She rolled her eyes. "I sure hope he meant it, or I'm in deep—" She looked at us and restrained an apparently forthcoming swear word. "I've got his mother's address right here." She patted the front pocket of her denim shirt.

"Anna!"

"Yes?"

"Your name is a palindrome."

"What's a palindrome? Is that a good thing? I sure hope so. I could sure use a good thing."

"It's a very good thing because my sister Grace and I," she tilted her head in my general direction, "are going to try to name as many palindromes as we can on our way to California and you, the first person who sat down next to us, has a name that's a palindrome. It's the same going forward and then backward. A-N-N-A."

Anna looked at Uny and angled her head slightly. "You must be smart young ladies to pick such a game."

"Thanks." She turned proudly toward me. "Last month, Grace finished getting a college degree online. We were homeschooled though. Some people ridicule us for that."

"Well, this palindrome thinks you're really smart and nice." Her eyes glistened, "I'm the first person to sit down next to you, and you're the first people to give me hope that my life can come back to some kind of normal after such a nasty rough patch. Um, why California? You goin' to visit family?"

"Yeah." Uny glanced over her shoulder at me again; this time as if to say, "Don't worry. I won't tell her about Pa." She patted my hand. "Yeah, we are. Our mamai's cousin has a motel by the ocean. We're going to go work there for a while."

"Mah-ma-i, is that like mommy?"

"Yes. We're Irish. It's kind of like the way Brits say mum."

"Mum! Palindrome!"

Anna grinned at me. "Maybe you'll become famous actresses in California."

Uny scoffed. "We're not going anywhere near Hollywood except to change buses. The motel is up north, closer to San Jose."

We waved good-bye to Anna in El Paso. I promised her, "I'll pray that you find your friend and don't end up homeless."

Her tired eyes gushed with water. "I'm sure glad I sat next to you two."

We moved our bags to the next bus. It wasn't crowded, and we were about to settle into the "same" seats on the new bus, but as we were boarding, I spotted a lecherous-looking dude undressing Uny with his eyes, so I tugged her arm and directed her to seats that were two rows behind him. I sat down, closed my eyes, and sent up the prayer I promised for Anna. I considered Uny's report to Anna about us going to work in a motel for a while. *Then what? Will we be hotel maids for the rest of our lives? What have I done? Where will we go from there?* I tossed around more self-condemnation before I finally escaped into numb sleep. We both slept most of the way to New Mexico.

The "hot seat" and the window seat next to it were empty from Lordsburg, New Mexico to Tucson. We slept on and off for a few more hours. In Tucson, a young woman boarded, intently examining the placement of each of her footsteps as she mounted the steps and proceeded up the aisle. She adroitly hid her face behind long, thick, shiny hair. She glanced up, searching for two adjacent, unoccupied seats. She spotted the two directly across from us. She tossed her backpack into the the window seat, and then expertly pulled up the armrest between the two seats before squishing her way over the armrest on the aisle. She glanced sheepishly at Uny and me. I think she saw me smile kindly before she dropped her eyes quickly as if to apologize for being overweight or for merely being alive. Catching the bus and climbing the stairs had left her breathing heavily.

Uny didn't launch into an enthusiastic greeting but merely bowed to her slightly with a caring smile. I admired my sister's sensitivity. This was not someone who wanted to blurt out her life story. There was heartbreaking pain in her young eyes. I prayed for her.

Her breathing calmed. She used her arms to heave herself a bit and shift her weight more comfortably into the two seats. She reached for her backpack and pulled out a bag of Doritos and a bottle of SmartWater. She screwed the top off the water bottle and raised the bottle as if to toast Uny and me. "I need to start somewhere," she proclaimed as she took a hearty sip. "I wasn't quite ready to give up both." She lifted the bag of Doritos. "Just the Pepsi." She grinned and took another sip.

Uny said, "Good for you. Are you starting on healthier choices?"

"Yes." She pulled the top of the chip bag open and handed it across the aisle. "Want some?"

"Don't mind if I do," Tilting her head toward me, Uny questioned with her eyes.

"Yes. Both of you. Please share with your sister."

"Pretty obvious, right? Yeah, this is my sister Grace. I'm Uny."

"Hi beautiful sisters, Grace and Uny."

The three of us nibbled on the spicy saltiness for a few minutes listening to the white noise of the smooth engine, rolling wheels, and the well-cushioned undercarriage of our air-conditioned Greyhound.

"Yeah, I need a lot of healthier choices. I basically did this to myself on purpose so my stepfather wouldn't find me attractive." She picked up one side of her ample bosom and bounced it. "Now that I no longer need to live in the same house with that creep, I'll try to find what's under this extra sixty pounds of camouflage." She took a deep breath.

Uny's voice was filled with sympathy. "Oh, I'm so sorry. That must have been horrible."

She looked down. "Yes." After a few more sips of water, she offered the Doritos bag to us and returned them to her backpack after we declined. "I'm not hungry anymore. I hope it lasts until I get to my dad's. He says his wife is a great, healthful foody, and she's a Jazzercise instructor. I'm hoping she can help me after I get there." Her eyes filled with tears.

It was logistically difficult to get close to her to hug her, so I searched instead for something to say that might comfort her. "Would you like us to pray for you?"

I saw heads jerk in my direction from the few seats in front of us. I imagined the people behind us were equally shocked.

She looked up from raccoon eyes deeply underscored by melting mascara. "Um. Sure. Do you mean right now or forever?"

I smiled. "Both." I took on the challenge to squeeze out in front of Uny, dropped to my knees in the aisle, put my hand on her arm, and whispered, "What's your name?"

She whispered back, "Josie."

I could see people nearby straining to hear us. My chest shuddered with a silent chuckle.

Josie noticed and responded likewise. "Are you sure?"

"Oh yeah. I'm tempted to shout it so the whole bus can hear, but I'll keep whispering. Dear Jesus, I know that You love Josie and You know everything that has caused her pain and brought her to this place and time. She wants to start a new life. Will You help her, please? And will You please remind me to pray for her every day?"

Josie was trembling. Uny tapped me on the shoulder and handed me two tissues, which I passed to Josie.

She wiped most of the remaining mascara from her face. "You're right, you know? He does know me and I know Him, but I haven't talked to Him for years. I asked Jesus into my heart at Vacation Bible School when I was little. I think my mom sent me there so she could have free babysitting for a week."

"May I hug you?"

She smiled through her tears. "Absolutely."

I got up from my knees and leaned into hair that smelled like lavender. She trembled as I hugged her the best I could in the crowded compartment. I stood back up. "Do you know the address at your dad's? We could stay in touch."

"How about my email address?"

"Yes! That's even better. I'm, um, changing mine." I looked over my shoulder at Uny to let her know I wasn't going to announce the details of our escape to a busful of Nosey Rosies. "It's a long story, but as soon as I have my new address, I'll send you an email."

Uny tapped me on my hip this time to move me out of the way. She handed a small pad of sticky notes and a pen to Josie. Josie wrote her full name, email address, and father's home address. It filled two little papers. I peeled them off, put them into my pocket, and handed the sticky note pack and pen back to Uny. Later, I was so glad we made the exchange in this primitive way, rather than type Josie's address into one of our iPads or into the pink cellphone.

Uny and would continue on the same bus to LA, but we had an hour layover in Phoenix from eleven thirty to midnight-thirty so we offboarded with Josie.

"He's a good guy, my dad. He's stayed in touch with me ever since the divorce. It was his idea to have me go with Mom because he felt a girl needed her mother. He always paid child support, which I think my mom treasured more than she did my custody. I only told my dad about Scott last night. He was crazy furious. He told my mom he was coming to get me, and he was going to call the authorities who would get there before he did. She told him she'd put me on this bus before he had a chance."

Uny and I each gave Josie an extended hug when her pa pulled up. Before she had a chance to introduce us, he took her into his arms for a long hug. Over her shoulder, I could see he was fighting tears. He put her bags into the back of his late-model Ford pickup and opened the passenger door for her. He offered his hand to assist her up. We waved to them as they pulled away.

Shortly after we reboarded and sat down, a dreadfully-thin couple boarded. I shivered when the man aggressively stared at me, and then assessed Uny. He pointed the woman with him into the window seat in front of me. Stale cigarette smoke and pungent, unwashed body aroma nearly caused me to gag. I checked behind me. The bus was filled to near capacity. We were trapped in our stinky surroundings. The man took the aisle seat directly in front of Uny.

Uny rolled her eyes but didn't bury her face. She wasn't going to let the smell deter her from making friends with another woman, who recently settled into "the Uny hot seat." Uny gave a friendly wave. "Hi."

"Hello. Are you twins? Your hair, the color, the curls, remind me of my daughter's when I last saw her." She sighed. "I've only seen pictures of her for the last ten years. She cut her long locks off a long time ago."

"Not twins, but sisters. I'm Uny. This is my big sister Grace." She shot me a mischievous smile over her shoulder and added. "We're gypsies."

"Gypsies? Really? I don't think I've ever met a gypsy."

I saw Creepy-smelly Dude in front of us peer through the crack in the seats to steal another glance at me. I glared back to discourage him, and he turned forward again.

"Well actually, we're Irish Travelers, but everyone has been calling us gypsies for so long, we gave up and joined in." Uny put her hands up in a brief gesture of surrender. "Are you going to California too?"

"Yes. A one-way ticket. I'm Hannah. How do you do?"

"Wow, Grace! Another palindrome!"

Hannah smiled knowingly. "Indeed. My name *is* a palindrome. I'd forgotten that it was. And you noticed, of course, that you just used another?"

Uny looked confused.

"Wow. You said wow." She studied the roof of the bus for a moment then shifted her gaze back to us. "Seems for a while I may have also forgotten who *I* was. I may need to find *me* again when I get to LA."

Uny looked bewildered, as any eighteen-year-old might, at such a philosophical observation.

I asked kindly, "Is that why you're going to California, to find a previous version of Hannah?"

She replied. "Or perhaps create a Hannah version 2.0. This is great. You girls are great. I thought this trip was going to be boring. Nothing boring about gypsies searching for palindromes though, right? I'm going to LA to live with my daughter for a while."

Uny smiled, "Do you only have one daughter?"

"Yes. She's my only family now that I'm leaving my husband."

"Oh, I'm so sorry."

"Don't be. He is a liar, a cheat, and there were plenty of other reasons why I should have left years ago." She seemed to sit up a little taller then she nodded wisely.

It seemed to me that Hannah was only in her mid-forties, but the deeply creased skin around her lips carried an expression of weariness. The corners of her mouth were turned down. Her clothes, though clean and neat, looked like they had once been expensive but were now tired, like her face. She wore slacks that didn't look all that comfortable, so I wondered if she was bringing only her best things to California with complete disregard for comfort. Someone had crisply ironed her worn, linen shirt. The buttons pulled at the front of her bosom as if the blouse had been purchased before weight gain. Her hair was straight, brown, and bobbed. Her eyes were also brown. They were filled with intelligence.

Ever positive Uny interjected, "Are you excited about your move? We are moving to California too, but we're going north to Monterey after LA."

I saw Creepy Dude twitch as if he were going to look at me again but decided not to risk my inevitable dirty look. He leaned close whispered something to his wife or whatever she was to him.

"I suppose I'm excited. My daughter has been trying to get me to come for a long time."

I was thinking that Hannah's daughter had probably surmised long ago that her mother was not being treated well by her stepfather.

Uny boldly asked as Uny was inclined to do, "Was the husband you are leaving your daughter's father?"

"No. Emily's dad passed away when she was small. I remarried very soon. Too soon. I was afraid to be alone raising Emily. I'm, or I was, an elementary school teacher. A great, rewarding job but lousy pay. I retired last year thinking I didn't need to work anymore." Hannah's eyes went flat as if bitterness had momentarily stolen life from them. "But, well, my story is similar to many other women who have married young then learned the harsh truth about fleeting looks and selfish men. He did love Emily though and was a good stepfather to her. He paid for an expensive education, sending her to Cal Tech where she got her doctorate and met a great guy."

"Is her husband an actor?"

Hannah smiled. "No. Emily thinks it's funny how people react when she tells them she's from California. Seems the rest of the world sees California chock-full of surfers and famous actors. Emily's husband is a physicist at Cal Tech where she went to school. She met him there. He's older than she is, but he treats her like a queen."

"So your daughter is a brainiac?"

"Yes. You could call her that. She married Michael after graduation and got a teaching credential. She teaches science at an inner-city school." Pride lifted Hannah's countenance. She looked about ten years younger when she smiled. She yawned and pulled her phone from her pocket and shook it to wake it up. "Oh gosh, no wonder I'm so tired. It's almost two AM. Will you excuse me? I'm going to try to dose for a while."

I nodded off but woke about a half an hour later when the bus stopped at Quartzsite, Arizona. Pretty much everyone stayed on the bus except the smelly couple in front of us and one other man. The three of them smoked in a designated area then reboarded, filling the immediate area with a renewed assault of stale cigarette smoke. I covered my nose with the collar of my hoodie and settled back leaning my head against the window and fell into a deep sleep. Uny's head was leaning against my shoulder.

I realized we were no longer moving. "Uny. Wake up. We're in LA. We need to transfer." I retrieved the tickets and the itinerary from my hoodie pocket, moved Josie's addresses that were stuck to the front of our itinerary, and attached them to the back. I studied our route.

Uny blinked a few times and stretched. "I have to go to the bathroom." She looked back toward the bathroom. "Everybody's gone!"

"Oh no! So is everything. Our carryon bags are gone. Someone must have slid them out while we were sleeping. Our baggage claim tickets, our IPads, my journal—our phone— our money!" *Zane's Poem.* "Come on. Let's hurry."

We stood, gaping at the empty hull beneath the bus. It was too late.

I asked Uny, "Do you have any money in your pockets?"

"Nothing. Everything was in my carryon with my iPad."

I closed my eyes and took a deep breath. "Oh gosh, the money, our pink phone, Shelta's address—all the numbers." *And Zane's.*

We were speechless for a moment, taking in our misfortune.

I pulled the itinerary and our remaining tickets from my pocket, "At least I had these on me." I fought emotion with a shaky, deep breath. "I guess there's only one thing to do now. Let's head north on the last bus. I don't suppose *you* remember the name of Cousin Shelta's motel?"

Uny looked miserable. "Sea Harbor? No, I don't think that's right."

"Are you okay?" I asked.

"No. I still have to go to the bathroom and I'm hungry."

"I am too. I'm so sorry." I hugged her. Let's go to the restroom, and then get on our next bus."

On the bus to Gilroy that would continue on to Monterey, Uny looked down at our itinerary. "Only a few stops left. We're supposed to get there around three. Hopefully, we'll remember the name of the motel by then, and maybe it's walking distance from the station."

Uny's stomach growled loudly. Mine replied at almost the same decibel.

I thought I felt as miserable as Uny looked, but I knew I wasn't when she whispered, "I started my period."

"What? Why didn't you tell me before we got on the bus?"

"Like that would help. What could you have done? The station was so huge and so crazy. And you were in such a hurry."

"I'm sorry. I was pretty mean. I was afraid the bus would leave before we found it."

"Well, I figured with no money, what could we do? I'll have just as much help here in the bus bathroom as we did at the station. I should be okay until this afternoon if we don't have to walk for miles." Uny's eyes brimmed with tears. "It's not quite as romantic being a gypsy as I thought it would be."

I patted Uny's arm to try to comfort her. "You're so silly."

At Gilroy station, we got off the bus in search of a drinking fountain but settled for using our hands as cups to drink tinny-tasting water from the restroom sink.

Uny whined, "I'm still thirsty. I wish I had that bottle of water that was in my backpack."

I was thinking the same thing. "Only a couple more hours to go. Are you gonna be okay or should I panhandle for Kotex before we get back on our bus?"

"I'm okay. Really. This is so over-the-top, ridiculously embarrassing already."

A stall door went bang against the restroom wall. "Oh, honey. Do you need some feminine products?" A large African American woman emerged from the bathroom stall. She was at least six feet tall.

Uny started to cry. "Someone stole our bags and all of our money in LA and our iPads and our cell phone."

"Now, now." She surrounded Uny with her arms, pulling her into an ample bosom. "They don't have machines here like they use to have everywhere but come with me. There's a little shop out there. We'll find what you need."

I asked, "Are you an angel?"

The woman laughed a hearty laugh. "Why yes, yes I am. I'm sent straight from Jesus and I'm going to buy you each a bottle of cold water in His name. Now hurry. I heard you say you need to reboard a bus."

"Thank you."

"Please. Just say, 'Thank you, Jesus.'"

We both smiled. "Thank you, Jesus."

Settled into the near-empty bus that continued on from Gilroy to Monterey, I tilted the water bottle from the angel. "I guess I better save some of this. I'm not sure how far we'll have to walk."

We disembarked onto a sidewalk. Our final destination wasn't even a station, merely a bus stop adjacent to an open plaza.

"Now what?" Uny asked.

Inhaling diesel exhaust, I waved my hand in front of my face. "For starters, let's get away from these buses." I took Uny's arm and pulled her into the plaza. "We need another angel."

She asked, "Which way should we go to find her?"

I looked over Uny's shoulder and pointed. "That way."

Uny turned and saw the sign that read, "Munras Grace Church."

I pressed down on the old fashioned brass tongue of the Church's front door and yanked. It jolted with a thud. Out of frustration, I repeated the thud two more times before I exclaimed, "Drat, drat, drat," one for each thud. "I guess there's no one here today." Uny looked like she was going to cry, so I put my arm around her. "Don't worry. We're still going to find an angel."

"Oh Grace, I hope you are right. And maybe a phone also?"

The door opened. "Hi. Can I help you? This ridiculous door. I heard you from my office. It always does that. It actually was open, but if you pull too soon—Oh!"

Either the woman saw Uny's forthcoming tears, or maybe we were both sending out obvious vibes of distress. "Come in. Please come in. My name is Tina. I'm the church secretary. How can I help you?"

I felt so relieved to follow Tina out of the bright sunlight into the coolness of an entry lined with portraits. I glanced at each briefly, noticing that beneath each of the portraits was a name or names of the people and the name of a city, some in a foreign country. *Missionaries*. We passed a wall with a window then turned into a doorway. "Please, have a seat." She motioned to two chairs separated by a small table. She began to settle herself in the chair behind a desk with a computer. When we didn't sit right away, she asked, "May I get you some water?"

Uny shook her head no then quickly nodded her head yes.

I offered explanation. "We've just arrived from riding buses from Texas. Our bags were stolen in LA. Our cell phone was in it. We were hoping we could use your phone, but—" I paused when I realized I didn't know where to call. I had not memorized Mamai's disposable cell number, and I was still unable to remember the name of the motel. I heard hysteria rising in my voice as I continued. "The phone numbers we need were in our cell phone. We were supposed to catch another bus to get to our cousin's motel, but we can't remember the name. The address, of course, was lost with the rest. My sister started her period, and a nice lady helped us in Gilroy—"

"Oh my! Of course, of course. You don't want to sit down, but you want some water. Yes, you can use the phone, and we'll figure out who to call, but first, come with me."

Tina got up from her desk and turned the opposite way from which we entered. We followed her into a walkway, past a large copy machine. She stopped briefly to grab two bottles of water from a box. She thrust one into each of our hands. She waved us to continue to follow her in into a narrow hallway, through an empty office, and out the door of that office into a large hallway. I saw entry doors standing open to a large, pew-filled sanctuary with an elevated stage in front. "This way." Tina turned away from the sanctuary doors then pushed open a large swinging door marked "Women."

At the end of the bank of stalls, Tina opened a narrow cupboard that was the same color and as tall as the stalls. The lower level shelves were crowded with toilet paper. From the eye level shelf, Tina grabbed a wrapped sanitary napkin, a tampon, and a box of baby wipes. She handed all of these to Uny and pointed to the box of baby wipes, "Please don't flush those. I'll be right back." She disappeared out of the bathroom door.

We settled on a bench in the entry located directly inside of the Ladies Room door and leaned back against a tile wall. I guzzled down half my water bottle. "Does it seem to you like she's been gone quite a while?"

"Yes. Do you suppose we should go?"

Tina came through the swinging door, holding a bright yellow plastic bag labeled, *Dollar General*. "Here." She pulled a package of underwear and some gray sweat pants out of the bag. "I think these are the right size or pretty close to it. I was once your size." She smiled and then turned to me. "You may not need them as desperately as your sister does, but there are three pair of panties in there." She pointed at the package. "Do you think you can find your way back to my office? I've ordered you a pizza. Should be here soon. I need to get back to cover the phones."

We sat in the two chairs across from Tina's desk, munching on the most delicious pizza I had ever tasted in my life, I decided not to mention anything about home to Tina. The thought of *home* caused my abdomen to ache. *Not anymore.* The harsh reality of leaving Mamai and our family continually tugged at my emotions. The shame of disrespecting Pa and our cultic customs crept in and sat down next to my heartache. But, the plight of women in our nomadic tribe needed someone to take up the cause, someone to behave valiantly, to fulfill a purpose larger than herself. My lofty ideas and dreams didn't warn me there would be day-to-day regret and uncertainty, or how I would be influencing my vulnerable sister. *What have I done by tearing us away from the security of Mamai's love?* But we had to leave. Our cultic customs were outrageously wrong. I took a deep breath and reaffirmed my decision and our actions. Mamai knew it too. It was the right thing to do, but I hadn't realized there would be so many repercussions and that I would feel so guilty. I rationalized that this was for the greater good. Perhaps as I change our future, we'll affect the fate of a few others. I cringed at the memory of those before me who had been traded for debt, as if they were a possession, not a person. I glanced at Uny. I knew the enthusiastic sense of adventure had faded for this mamai's girl. The anguish of our actions was becoming real. I wanted to talk to Mamai but couldn't risk calling her original cell phone or the home phone. I was determined to stick with the plan. We needed to find Shelta.

I interrupted my thoughts to ask Tina, "Have you ever heard of Sea Harbor Motel?"

"Hmmm, no." She started typing on her keyboard. "No. There is no Sea Harbor Motel or Hotel in Monterey." Mumbling to herself, she continued to click, then type, then click, click, click.

As if the water and magic pizza finally woke up my brain, I exclaimed, "Seal Harbor! Not Sea Harbor, and I don't think it's in Monterey but nearby."

Tina typed and clicked then said, "Yes! Seal Harbor Inn. Pacific Grove, not Monterey." She turned and smiled at us. "No, please don't look so distressed. Pacific Grove is almost the same as Monterey. The boundary is next to the Monterey Bay Aquarium. It's only a few miles from here."

I was relieved but also not thrilled that if we couldn't reach Shelta, or if Shelta was unable to come to get us, we still had a few miles to go on foot. I supposed that wouldn't be so bad since we no longer had luggage. "Is there a phone number?"

"Of course." Tina picked up the phone, looked her screen, handed the handset to me, and punched in the numbers."

"Seal Harbor Inn, this is Honey."

"Is Shelta available?" I don't know why I was relieved that Hogan Crosby didn't answer. In spite of Mamai's description of his love for women, I was harboring an ominous fear of him.

"She might be, but I'm checking in guests at the moment. Do you wish to hold or may I have Shelta call you back?"

"Sure, just a sec." I looked at Tina, "What is your number here?" I repeated the number to Honey as Tina gave it to me in segments, "Please tell Shelta her cousins Grace and Uny are at Munras Grace Church in Monterey." Fighting disappointment and tears, I hung up the phone.

"Are you okay?"

Tina's kindness shredded my resistance. I began to cry openly. "I'm sorry." I wiped my sniffles with my whole hand then rubbed my nose viciously with a circular motion. It was not one of my more ladylike moves. I expected Tina to say it was all going to be okay, instead, I was surprised by her response.

She handed me the whole box of Kleenex from her desk. "Go ahead and cry. You're exhausted. You've been robbed of all your belongings, and your little sister's been stricken by our female nemesis at the worst possible moment. But, this is almost over." She got up and opened her arms wide enough for both of us. We both stood up and, even though I was acutely aware of how stinky we were, we accepted her offer and snuggled into a tearful group hug. I interrupted our hug to pull out several tissues, handed some to Uny, and we each continued to rest our wiped faces on the shoulders of our second angel.

The phone rang.

"Munras Grace, this is Tina. Yes. They're right here." She smiled and handed me the phone.

CHAPTER EIGHT

Cooey Devlin

Cooey Devlin's grip caused his knuckles to turn white as he crushed a box of garbage bags. How dare they leave in the middle of the night? He was furious that Grace and Uny snuck out of their rooms without leaving a clue to their destination, and they had left their mother incapacitated. His normally too-chatty wife had hardly spoken to him since they woke up three days ago. He drew a black plastic bag from the box and furiously jammed in as many of Grace's jeans, tops, and dresses without regard to how they would inevitably wrinkle. He ignored the sweet little faces staring at him from the curio shelf in Grace's room and dropped her dolls one by one into the dark oblivion of the next black bag. He mumbled to himself. "St. Vincent de Paul's will find someone who will appreciate this stuff. Ungrateful imps." *Clever and calculating, those two, or probably just Grace. Yes. It would have been Grace that would have known not to take the phones. Rats! He could have tracked them.* He turned to see Danee standing next to Grace's dresser. Her eyes were red and swollen. She looked at him and then looked at Grace's jewelry box.

He tried to tame the undertone of anger that was permeating his every thought, his every move, and he knew it would come through in his voice. "What? Why are you in here, Danee?"

"Um. I heard the noise and wondered what it was."

He had to unclench his back molars to answer. "I'm cleaning out these rooms. They don't deserve any of it."

She looked down at the bag with a doll's foot sticking out, "But Grace loves those dolls."

"Well, Grace should have thought about the things she loves and the people she supposedly loves before she pulled her disappearing act, shouldn't she?"

Danee's tears began to flow openly. Her voice was nasally. "Well, I guess. So, don't you want Grace and Uny to ever come back?"

He hadn't really considered whether he wanted them to come back; he was so frustrated at his loss of power; his obsession had turned into revenge. He could no longer control them, but he could remove all traces of their rebellion.

Danee pulled a few tissues from the box by Grace's bed, blew her nose noisily, and returned to the dresser. She lifted the lid on Grace's jewelry box and picked up her garnet necklace. "I'm surprised she didn't think to take this. Are you going to give this to St. Vincent de Paul too?"

Cooey remembered giving each of the girls their birthstone necklaces when they turned ten. For the first time since he woke three days ago to Anita telling him they were gone, he was experiencing an emotion other than anger. He had indefinable pain that no one could see. It was as if he were bleeding inside. His thoughts shifted to their loss of Johan, he admitted to himself that he did didn't want Grace and Uny's act of disobedience to be irreversible. He fought a tightness welling up and gruffly cleared his throat. "Do you want Grace's jewelry? You can have it. You can have Uny's too." He wondered if she was too afraid to answer until she spoke. Then he realized she was gathering her courage to say more than yes.

Softly she asked, "May I please have their dolls too?"

He was tempted to punish her for her impudence. He didn't want to soften any of his spiteful plans to clear out all traces of Grace and Uny, but Danee's sweetness and seeing Grace's garnet necklace lanced through his anger. "Yeah. Okay. Here." He handed her the bag of dolls. "Go get Uny's before I get back up here. I'm going downstairs for a while. Gonna check my email." After he dragged the first three bags downstairs and tossed them into the back of his SUV, he sat down heavily into his massive desk chair.

No emails. No calls on the home phone. No messages from the network of friends he'd hailed to be on the lookout. Nothing.

His frustrated thoughts felt tangled. The scrawny branches of the white oak sapling outside the den window threw shadows on the floor of his den, twisting darkness into the golden glow of the hardwood. He pressed his thumb into the wooden whorl on the top desktop that seemed to match his thumbprint perfectly and held it there as he had so many times before. It calmed the sting in his eyes and the hurt in his heart as he connected with this solid, unemotional, inanimate object. What could he do? Technically, his daughters were adults so the police wouldn't help. It was obviously not an abduction. Could Grace have possibly guessed he offered her as a wife to Murph? Even if she did and she objected, how could she forsake her heritage and defy him, Cooey Devlin, after all his generosity? He looked around the mansion in his mind's eye. When they stopped being nomads to settle as house dwellers, he provided comfort, security, and even extravagance. Still pondering she how could have pulled this off and why she took Uny, he picked up his coffee cup and headed to the kitchen for his fourth refill. Anita was vacuously staring out the window from her spot at the kitchen table.

"Oh. Nita. There you are. You feeling better?"

The only thing worse than her ignoring him by gazing out the window was the fear that she would actually start talking about her feelings or worse, expect him to talk about his.

After a moment, she droned a monotone reply, "No. I'm not feeling better and it doesn't seem as if I ever will."

"Don't look at me like that, woman. You think this is my fault?"

She turned her gaze back to study the fountain flowing in the midst of the rose garden. "The roses aren't doing well, Cooey. I think it's too hot in Texas for roses. Maybe we should rethink our landscaping. These tiny trees we've planted can't grow fast enough to spare our garden from the afternoon sun."

"Nita! How you can think about trees and flowers at a time like this?" He brushed his hands through the top of his once-thick mane, cringed when he felt the bald spot in the back, but then turned his attention back to his angst. "I gave those girls everything to make them happy. You know that. All the new-fangled technical gadgets, big TVs with a million channels and streaming options, nice clothes, good food, the privilege to drive our cars."

"All so they could do your bidding, right? You expected them to live their lives entirely for you."

Cooey turned his back on her, clenched the handle of the coffee pot, counted to ten in his head, and slowly poured coffee. She was right, but he was also right. Right to expect it. They were *his* family. They were raised to give him full honor, respect, and obedience. He turned back to his wife and nearly growled, "I still can't believe they dared to betray me. Besides that, how did they pull it off?" He thought he saw Anita flinch. *No, it can't be. She's just distraught.* More tenderly, he suggested, "Why don't you go upstairs and take a nice long bath?"

"Are you saying I stink?"

Her curtness shocked and confused him. *What's going on?* "No, but it has been a few days since you've done anything nice for yourself." He wouldn't dare admit aloud that she *was* beginning to smell a little ripe. "If you don't feel like a bath, go on up and take a rest. Danee and I will fix dinner."

"Really?"

He smiled, thinking he finally had this exceedingly awkward situation under control, "Really."

"Has it occurred to you to ask Danee if she *wants* to fix dinner? We both know that 'you and Danee,' means Danee."

"Listen to me, woman. I don't know where all this disrespect is coming from, but I've had enough. Yes. Danee will still do as I direct her. Apparently, though, *you* are disinclined."

Danee appeared at the kitchen door and asked with her still nasally voice. "Did I hear my name?"

Anita rose from her spot, padded across to Danee, and took her into her arms. "Danee, my sweet girl, I'm going upstairs to take a bath. Would you mind helping Pa fix our dinner? Fry up some little strips of bacon to go with some frozen green beans." She pointed to the freezer drawer beneath twin refrigerator doors. She turned to glare at him, "Teach your Pa how to make Kraft mac and cheese. There are a few boxes in the pantry."

Cooey thought, *Good!* At least one person was not out of his control. Danee could pick up the slack for her worthless mamai. He felt proud of himself for giving her Grace's and Uny's jewelry and dolls. At least he had *one* good daughter.

CHAPTER NINE

Seal Harbor Inn

Thud, thud, thud came from the church's entryway. Tina said, "That's probably your cousin." She escorted us to the frustrating door and opened it.

Both Uny and I exclaimed, "Shelta?"

Shelta was slim; her skin was clear and accented by expertly applied makeup. Her once long, frizzy hair was still auburn but now a stylish medium length, shimmering and straight. She wore classy slacks with a silky, flowy ivory blouse. She embraced us both, kissed Uny, kissed me, and stepped back. "Welcome to California!" She reached out to take Tina's hand, "Thank you so much." She looked at the yellow plastic bag in my hand. "How much do we owe you?"

"The church has a fund for these kinds of emergencies. We've got this." Tina smiled at us. "Oh, wait here, just a sec." She hurried to her office and back and then handed me a large envelope. "Here's some of our church's introductory material. It has the times of our services and everything. Please come visit us again. We don't usually serve pizza, but we've been known to serve feast-worthy food. There's church potluck in a few weeks and a barbecue in the church courtyard next month. It's on the calendar." She tapped the envelope. "God bless you."

The strap of Shelta's classy, crossbody, leather handbag left her hands free to take each of ours. We walked three abreast back to the courtyard where the bus had dropped us. We crossed to a parking lot, containing her burnished silver Cadillac. "I'm so glad you're here. Your mamai's been calling all day. She knows you're okay now. I called her as soon as I hung up with you. She'll call again when the coast is clear." She raised one eyebrow. "You had pizza?"

"Yes," I was still marveling at Shelta's makeover. "Gosh, you look great!"

"Well, thank you. I made some huge changes when Hogan took me in. He said he didn't care; he liked me the way I was, but I started going to the gym with him after Ryker was born. I saw him there, flirting with all the girls." She scoffed. "*All* of them. Young, old, fit, far from fit. He takes classes with them pretty much every day. Seeing his open acceptance of them, helped me realize that he really *did* like me just the way I was, so I liked me better too. For some reason, his acceptance spurred me on to take advantage of the California lifestyle. It's so easy here to get healthy food and get fit. And though Hogan *said* he didn't care what shape I was, he definitely took a keener interest in me when I slimmed down." She grinned as she turned the car onto a street that had dropped from sight momentarily. The Cadillac plunged down a hill.

Involuntary squeals bubbled up from Uny and me when we caught our first sight of the Pacific Ocean. It looked like a huge platform of blue diamonds with a thick fog bank a few miles away. Then I realized it was land, not fog. From the map I'd studied before it was stolen, this was the Monterey side of the bay, and that fog-like ridge floating in the distance was Santa Cruz. The car turned parallel to the shoreline. Ocean View Boulevard was flanked with white surf, rock islands, and twisted trees that had been bent into sweeping shapes by years of onshore flowing wind. Almost involuntarily, I took a deep breath before saying, "Oh, so beautiful."

Shelta pushed a button. The Cadillac's windows slid into the door. A faint breeze blowing off the land on the left side of the car carried a heavy scent of pine, sweet and sharp, coming in warm puffs through the cool salt smell of the sea. All so lovely, but I felt a chill and shivered.

"Yes, so beautiful. I squealed the first time I saw it too. I walk along the bay every day, even when it's cold and foggy, at least for a few minutes. To this day, I still have that inner squeal of delight when I step out the Inn's front door." Shelta turned on her left blinker, stopped the car, and waited for traffic. She waved her arm toward the surf crashing and splashing on the rock islands. Here we are." I didn't question the obvious pride in her tone. "This is the Seal Harbor Inn view."

I asked "Is that the birds? They sound like they are barking."

"No, that's the sound of baby seals reminding their mamais to feed them."

I smiled then and found myself smiling thereafter almost every time I heard their barking cries.

Uny exclaimed, "Cute guy alert!" On the porch of the building ahead of us, a tall, broad-shouldered man stood staring toward the breaking waves. His brown wavy hair was neatly cut on the sides. He turned toward us and waved. Even filtered through the Cadillac's tinted windshield, his eyes were apparently clear blue.

"That's Drake. He works for us. Does all the handyman stuff, even though Hogan probably could. Yes, he's definitely cute." She turned left, then right into the Inn's driveway and parked in a carport. "Okay. First things first. Hogan wants to say, 'hi' and then you get to take showers."

"Yay!"

Uny asked, "Can I go first?"

"Of course."

"After your mamai calls, we're headed to Target for clothes, jammies, underwear, and toothbrushes. You look cold."

"I am. We're not in Texas anymore. I'd like to get a hoody that's warmer than this one. I'll wear it until I get used to this ocean breeze."

Uny rubbed the outsides of her arms, "Right? Me too. Not sure I've felt this cool outside of air-conditioning for a long time."

"You've got it. Two warm jackets added to your shopping list right now. Oh, and a phone. Your mamai wants you to get another phone right away. Actually, would both of you like one? We'll be paying you to work for us so—"

We both replied, "Yes, please."

"Since we'll be paying you back, may we get smartphones? I made a friend on one of our buses. I pulled Josie's sticky notes from my pocket. I have her email address. I'd like to set up a new email."

"Of course. We'll cut Target short and only get what's essential for the next few days. Then, we'll stop at AT&T. I'll add your new phones to my plan."

The apartment door swung wide as we approached it. My first impression of Hogan Crosby was that he was old, with a leathery form of handsomeness, and quite a bit shorter than Shelta. He had thick, mostly white hair. A small, distinguished dark streak started at the center of his forehead and faded into gray. There were other bits of dark hair on the back of his head. I remembered Mamai saying that Aislyn, like Shelta, had also been taller than he was. He had dark eyes and wore expensive, comfortable clothes. I would learn later that he could be an advertisement for a men's designer clothes line called Tommy Bahama. His voice was a bit gruff, lacking the softness, nuances, and humor of our fellow Irish folk, but his words were kind. "Welcome, girls. Welcome to our home." As he spoke, I wasn't sure who he was talking to. It seemed like he was looking over my left shoulder. I felt as if I should take a step to the left to correct his line of sight. I would learn that stepping into what seemed to be his line of sight would not have helped. This quirky habit had its origin in insecurity, or perhaps guilt, that hindered his ability to make direct eye contact. "It's nice to have two more daughters. Come in. Come in. This is Ryker." A boy, who looked about five or six, peered at us through eyes the same brilliant turquoise as Shelta's and gave us a huge, partially toothless smile. "It's nice to have a son too, though." He ruffled the boy's curly hair. Hogan Crosby's expression was the most indecipherable thing about him; his smiling face spoke of kindness, but his eyes held the threat of damnation.

The apartment was comfortable but cavelike. I would learn later that it was the only two-story dwelling in the Inn and housed the only fireplace and chimney on the premises. Dense curtains blocked the light. Dark, heavy furniture rested on plush, brown carpet. A ropelike wall-hanging was to the left of the fireplace. An unidentifiable black and white photo or print was on the right. In the dim light, it looked like a barren tree with big, black birds hovering in the branches. Maybe crows or ravens? Directly across from the fireplace sat a tufted, brown leather couch. The décor's ominous darkness didn't fit Shelta's new classy style. Crosby must have been the decorator.

Shelta gave us a little background on the Inn as she settled us into a simple but immaculate room with two double beds. It had been built in the nineteen fifties when laws required architects and builders to design and build bathrooms on outside walls containing windows. Our tiny window, like the rest we could see from our room, was more the size of a large vent. It was placed so high on the bathroom wall, a step stool was required to clean it. Apparently during the fifties, shower stalls were rare so each of the Inn's rooms had the advantage of a bathtub. Our room was directly next door to the Crosby apartment. "I know you had pizza, but I bet you'll be hungry again soon. Come back when you're ready." She pointed to her front door. "Here." She handed each of us a bottle of water. "Clean yourselves up as best as you can with what you've got and rest a bit. I'll come to get you straight away if your mamai calls. We'll go out for those clean clothes and your new phones soon."

After we returned from our whirlwind shopping trip, we settled at Shelta and Crosby's table for a delicious dinner of fish and vegetables.

"I didn't know I liked fish."

Uny agreed with me, "Me neither."

Looking at the bowl of spinach, Ryker asked, "Can I eat some of that grass?"

Shelta gave Uny and I a you'll-get-used-to-it smile. "Sure, only its sautéed spinach, not grass." She put a spoonful on his plate.

Hogan looked over my left shoulder and stated, "Everything tastes good when you're hungry, even fish."

Shelta pointed toward the Monterey Bay. "Especially fish that was swimming out there a few hours ago."

"Wow! Really? Who caught it?"

"Not us, but when I go to the market and it says, 'catch of the day,' it really means it was caught today, unlike restaurant menus across the United States that erroneously brandish that phrase around." Shelta grinned.

Hogan looked over Uny's left shoulder and suggested, "Hey, it's almost sunset. Why don't you take a walk before you go to bed? I'm sure those beds in your room are calling to you, but go watch the waves for a few minutes so when you hear them throughout the night, you'll also see them in your dreams."

And dream we did. We were so pooped. We didn't chat or try to process any of what had happened in the past two days. Shelta had insisted on washing our new clothes. Our new jammies were still warm from the dryer. We had hardly brushed our teeth and put our heads on our pillows before soft snoring from Uny's bed tipped me off that she was sound asleep. I wasn't far behind, but I took time to pray for Josie as I promised. I'm not sure I made it through the rest of my intended list, but I spoke the names of Mamai, Pa, Danee, Billy, and Uny. I remembered our palindromes, Anna and Hannah, and thanked Jesus for our two angels. I pressed the tears tightly back as I prayed for Zane. Before I could begin the conversation I needed to have with God about the consequences my actions would have on my family, especially Uny, I slipped into a welcome, comfortable sleep.

In my groggy state, I wasn't sure what woke me. I glanced at the motel digital clock to see it was only ten forty-one. Then I heard an angry voice coming through the wall behind the headboard. Then a loud bang. I rolled out of bed and put my ear to the wall.

Crosby's voice was raised, but I could only distinguish a word or two. "Don't you," And, "No!" And I think, "I'm not going to stand for it!" In between, I heard soft indecipherable replies from Shelta.

I lay back down and pondered this. Pa adhered to the creepy, old fashion ways of treating women like property, but I had never heard him yell at Mamai as Crosby was yelling at Shelta. If my parents had ever argued, apparently we were spared from being spectators. I wondered what the banging noise could be and thought there may have been a first bang that woke me. As tired as I was, it was hard to return to sleep. After a while though, it got quiet, and I surrendered my worry to the night.

Our first morning at Seal Harbor, Shelta let us sleep in, but she made it clear that it would not always be so. She wanted us up, clean, dressed, and at her breakfast table by eight thirty every morning. Ivy arrived at six to make coffee in the front office for the motel guests, and then she came to Shelta's apartment so Shelta could go to the front office to serve the guests. Four days a week, it was Ivy who got Ryker bathed, dressed, and settled him at the breakfast table to eat the hot breakfast she prepared for him. Shelta asked Ivy to also make breakfast for Uny and me. On Friday, Saturday, and Sunday, Honey showed up at five-thirty to make coffee, but she stayed at the desk in the front office. On those three days, Shelta got Ryker ready for his day and made our breakfast. On Sunday, we all went to church. It was our first time to attend a church that wasn't Catholic. When the pastor stepped up to the podium, he said, "Men are walking down the aisles with Bibles marked to the passage we'll be studying this morning. Raise your hand if you'd like one, and if you don't own a Bible, it is a gift from the Lord." Uny and I looked at each other and smiled. I held the Gift next to my heart for a moment before opening to the passage.

Monday was supposedly Shelta's full-day off. Ivy was back making breakfast for all of us, and although Shelta was home, Ivy helped Ryker get dressed. Several times a week, Ivy also did the Crosby household laundry. Whenever Shelta needed her to, Ivy took Shelta's dry cleaning with her when she left for home and returned it several days later, covered in sheer plastic. I took charge of our personal laundry and blended it into the weekly schedule.

Shelta, not Crosby, merged Uny and me into the rotation of motel maids that cleaned rooms, folded motel laundry, kept the motel laundry room clean, scoured the thirty-cup coffee pot, restocked the racks with brochures, maps, and copies of the local newspaper, and vacuumed and dusted the front office. This was a room at the end of the front deck where guests were greeted, checked in, checked out, helped themselves to free coffee, and were served if needed. It overlooked Ocean View Boulevard which ran adjacent to the breathtaking Monterey Bay. The premium ocean-front rooms continued along that same deck and were topped with a second story of rooms with an even more spectacular view. A second two-story building jutted off along the back parking lot, in the shape of an "L," perpendicular from the ocean-front rooms. Uny's and my room was on the ground floor of the wing that didn't face the Bay, but we could always smell it and hear it, especially in the evening. Though named Ocean View Boulevard, it was actually a tiny road, used primarily in the daytime. After dark, most travelers were couples walking to or from Cannery Row, often romantically cuddled closely together to keep each other warm in the cool ocean breeze. A second, larger office was above our room. It shared a wall with the second story of the manager's apartment, also in the non-ocean-front wing. Shelta told us that before we came, there was only one person she trusted to clean the upstairs office, but now that I was here, she would trust me also. I was touched by her faith in me. Uny didn't seem to notice she was excluded, or perhaps she didn't care.

We joined Crosby, Shelta, and Ryker for dinner each night. Uny and I had full kitchen privileges during the day to make lunch, tea, or snacks. I volunteered to cook a couple of evenings each week. I also volunteered to help do the grocery shopping. Shelta promised she'd help us both make appointments at the California DMV as soon as possible. Until then, we could legally drive their Jeep with our Texas driver's licenses. Fortunately, mine had been in a little plastic sleeve tucked into my hoodie pocket when our backpacks and luggage disappeared. Uny's had been stolen with the rest.

"Not the Cadillac?"

Shelta quipped, "No, I'm sure that's illegal, Grace, even with a California license." We all chuckled.

We easily fell into a routine. Unlike Uny, I loved to work. I pushed away my thoughts of home, Mamai, Pa, Danee, and Billy. And Zane. I wished for the millionth time I could tell Zane I lost my phone. I'm sure he must have figured it out when I didn't answer it or worse, when someone else did. He knew he had the right number because of the way I sent it to him in a text that last day we were together. That wretched phone, though not a smartphone, was smarter than I was. I wished, wished, wished I had memorized his number. I didn't dare go on Instagram, Snapchat, or Facebook. Pa was not social media savvy, but I'd bet a dollar to a donut he thought of that immediately and enlisted someone to start trolling.

Ryker was homeschooled. When he was done with his lessons, I would often take him with me to grocery shop. Normally, without complaint, the boy would eat anything. He sampled everything offered at Costco demonstration tables. "You almost didn't get to come with me today, Ryker."

"Yeah. Now I only have a half-bad attitude."

"Really?"

"Yeah. Mamai sent me to my room this morning and told me I had to find a better attitude." He explained with his arms and hands. "This is a whole bad attitude and this is a half-bad attitude."

"So she let you come because you've only got a half-bad attitude now?"

"Yes." He stretched his arms as far as he had before to explain. "Only this much, but now that she let me come with you, it's not even half-bad anymore."

"I see. All good now."

He tilted his head toward the cracker piled high with canned chicken, knowing the demonstration lady had to give it to me to give to him." I handed him the cracker. "I'm proud of you for having a good attitude now."

"Thanks." He crunched into the cracker.

After restocking the front desk with copies of the latest issue of the local newspaper, *Monterey Pine*, the rest of the coffee supplies, and tidying up the coffee area, I paused at the rail on the veranda to watch the swells and waves across the street. A seagull laughed at me as a huge wave crashed over the tiny island of rock twenty feet out from the sand and rock beach. A breathtaking spray of white froth soared high above the top of the rocks then waterfalls trickled down twisting into the foam beneath. Another swell, wave, crash, spray, foam, and gurgle. I was mesmerized.

A deep voice jerked me out of my trance. "You know if you go across the street, and then walk down about fifty yards, the seals are birthing. There are pups spread out all over that beach. In fact, listen, you can hear them barking."

I tuned my ear to filter the sound of passing cars. A gull squealed; a crow chuckled from the cypress above us, but then I heard the pups and smiled. "We heard them the first day we arrived." I looked up into clear, slate blue eyes of the man who had been standing right here when we arrived at Seal Harbor. The one who Uny dubbed "cute-guy." He was even cuter up close but older than my first impression. Deep creases etched the corners of his eyes and his tanned forehead. He had to be at least six two, probably more like six three or four, and he smelled fantastically clean. He had the look of physical health, for which he apparently worked and maintained. "Hi. I'm Grace." I put out my hand. "Shelta told us that you are Drake, the handyman."

His huge hand gently enveloped mine, and he bowed slightly, "Drake, the handyman, at your service."

I smiled. "So, do we need repairs today?"

We both turned toward the water. His hands gripped the rail. A band of white on his left ring finger starkly contrasted with his otherwise bronze hands. "Not sure yet. I come every Monday to be a hawkeye, check in with Shelta to see if any of the guest room maintenance feedback cards reported anything, then I make a punch list. I come back on various other days to take care of the list, depending."

"This is Shelta's day off."

"Yes, but Monday usually has fewer guests and Shelta rarely, totally takes a day off." He grinned.

"So, I've only been here a week or so, but it seems to me that Shelta runs this business, not Crosby, right?"

"Yeah, but she's good." The creases at the corners of his eyes deepened. "She runs it, and yet he thinks *he's* running it.' He pointed to the right. "Let me get this straight. You've been here over a week, and you haven't gone down the street that way to see the baby seals?"

"Um. Yeah. I suppose that's true. We've been walking the opposite way to Lover's Point."

"Can you go now?"

"I guess, but I should probably let someone know I'm taking a break."

"Okay, let's go tell Shelta I'm here and ask permission for you to take a break."

Uny came up behind him, looking like the Mock Shocked Emoji. She composed her face before Drake turned around. "Drake, this is my sister, Uny. Uny, this is Drake, the handyman."

They each nodded.

"Drake says there are seal pups down the beach the opposite direction from the way we've been taking our walks. We were just going to ask Shelta if it's okay to take a break. Come with us."

The blob-like bodies of various sizes were everywhere. Some of the mamai seals were returning from feeding themselves in the sea. They floated onto the beach then wiggled and inched their shiny, rubber-like forms along the sand until they lay aside their waiting pups. Most of the babies on the beach were heartily sucking their dinner. Once again, I was mesmerized.

Uny looked distressed. "That tiny baby doesn't have a mamai."

"Maybe she'll be back soon."

A man's voice behind me answered, "Nope. I don't think so, sometimes the mothers don't have enough milk so they abandon their pups." The owner of the voice had on a yellow vest with orange stripes across his chest. His tag, in large letters, had his name, "Charlie," and in teeny letters above his name a lengthy sentence that ended with "Fish and Wildlife."

"Why not?" I could hear the distress in my sister's voice.

"We've been watching him for a few days. He's been abandoned for a while."

Drake pointed to the barrier. "You don't want us to help him either, right? That's why you put up this extra fencing?"

"Right. Warning signs, like that one," he pointed, "are always around, but these temporary fences go up during April and May, just in case people can't read, or they disregard the plea to leave the seals and their birthing routines alone. One improper intervention can cause lots of birthing moms to suddenly miscarry."

"Oh no!" Now I was distressed. "Won't one of the other mamais feed her if hers doesn't come back?"

Charlie asked, "Her?"

I smiled at him and tilted my head, "Why not?"

The pup cried out as if she knew we were talking about her. Uny's eyes glistened.

"No. They only feed their own pups. We'll keep an eye on him, er her. If she's still there in a few days, we may intervene and take her to the Marine Mammal Center."

"Let's name her Loosey."

"Lucy?" Charlie looked amused.

"Yeah." Uny wiped her nose with the back of her hoody sleeve. "Loosey, because she's on the loose without her mamai." She looked at me. "Kinda like us."

At the dinner table that evening, Shelta served some slices of grilled chicken breast, but mostly we ate a lot of crunchy, perfectly roasted vegetables.

Uny whined, "I don't know why Fish and Wildlife has to wait. They need to take Loosey to the mammal center really soon. Charlie says they've been watching for days. Loosey's mamai came once a few days ago, but there was no milk for Loosey."

Crosby looked over Uny's left shoulder. "Well that's the way life is you know. Dying is part of living for man and beast."

Ryker's head jerked up from his plate where he had just picked up a spear of asparagus with his fingers, "Huh?"

"Hogan Crosby!" I'm sure Shelta saw the disapproving, almost cruel, glare that he hurled over her left shoulder like a rock.

Uny's hoody sleeve had had an eventful day. She dabbed her nose with it. "Yabut, we could help her. People, I mean. They won't let me help her, not that I could. I just wish they would take her to the mammal center and feed her with a bottle, and then teach her how to fish."

"Now, now Uny." Crosby patted her arm. "Fish and Wildlife will step in on time. Don't worry. Keep going down there every day. You'll see." He shot another aggressive glare over Shelta's shoulder before whining, "I'm not heartless, you know. I'm just being realistic." He lowered his head, as if he were expecting us to feel sorry for him at Shelta's implied insult.

CHAPTER TEN

Emails with Josie

Grace to Josie:

Hi Josie. I have email at last! How are you?

Uny and I had quite an "adventure." I guess that's what I could call it. All of our stuff was stolen. Fortunately, I had your sticky notes stuck to our itinerary and the tickets for the final leg of our journey, all in my pocket. As I think about our trip, having those essential things in my pocket was not the only thing we have to thank God for. Two wonderful women, who Uny and I call "angels" helped us along the way. The first angel even said not to thank her, but to say, "Thank you Jesus." The other angel gave us food, water, clean clothes, and helped us to find our way to our new "home."

We are at a cousin's motel in Pacific Grove. I still can't believe how beautiful it is here. With all the traveling my family did when I was a child, I had only had glimpses of the ocean on the gulf coast. We are in a building that sits RIGHT ON the Monterey Bay! Everyone just calls it "the ocean." Even the street we are on is called, Ocean View Boulevard, which is actually not a boulevard at all. It's a quiet, two-lane road that people use to get close to the beaches.

Uny and I are going to stay here at least for a while and work for our cousin as motel maids.

So please tell me how it is living with your father. As I promised, I've been praying for you.

Josie to Grace:

Hi Grace! It's great to hear from you. I'm doing very, very well. As I promised myself, I've been eating better (and less) and exercising. It is so easy to live with Dad and Kris. She enrolled me in school for the next semester, but ordered a bunch of home school material and told me I could finish up this year without making what she called a "grand entrance" as the new kid so late into the school year. She is so cool.

So, you mentioned it was a long story. Anything you want to share about why you moved to California and changed your email address?

Grace to Josie:

Oh gosh, the story is so long so I'll quote Inigo Montoya in The Princess Bride. "Let me sum up."

Basically, we ran away. My mamai helped us though. We are what most people call gypsies, but we are Irish Travelers and what I consider a cult. My pa arranged for me to marry the FATHER of my love interest, Zane. The people in our culture often have multi-generational family living arrangements. So at least for a while, Zane would have lived in the same house with his pa with me as his pa's wife!

So, because Uny may have been next in line for the same, ridiculous arrangement (except for the love interest), she came with me.

I've always wanted to make a difference in the world. Not just wanted to, I feel destined to. I'm not sure if I'll accomplish this as a motel maid though. LOL. And yes, don't worry, I'm not fooling myself. This was much more of a selfish move than an altruistic one. What I know for sure is, I didn't want to marry Zane's pa!

CHAPTER ELEVEN

Surrogate Brother

Hanging out with Ryker was like being with my little brother Billy, whom I had deserted and I missed awfully, almost as much as I missed Mamai. I remembered what Mamai told us about Shelta being pregnant before she married Crosby and wondered who Ryker's father might be, thinking it could be an outsider. Someone within our clan culture would have been guilted into stepping up to marry Shelta, or at least support her child unless—he was already married. Even then, he would be guilted into supporting them. Ryker looked like Shelta in the shape of his face and those amazing, turquoise eyes. He had her auburn hair that was very much like Mamai's, Uny's, and mine. He also got her remarkable caterpillar eyebrows with a phenomenal ability to curve independently into quirky expressions.

He expressed some of the silliest things. The first day I sat down on the floor with him. Because he was barefoot, I took off my shoes.

He studied one of my feet for a minute, then studied one of his. "Your thumb toe is bigger than my thumb toe."

I giggled.

Ryker was fascinated when I stepped into the kitchen. As a working mother, Shelta mostly served purchased, healthy, pre-prepared, ready-to-heat or ready-to-toss-together meals.

But, her fully-equipped kitchen made it easy for me to make dinners from scratch.

"Want to watch?" I pulled a chair up to the countertop and gave him a hand up.

He spotted the food in front of him. "I don't want you to make sausage and potatoes for dinner."

"Hmmm... Well, what are *you* going to make for dinner?"

"I can't make dinner!"

"Why can't you make dinner?"

"I don't have enough hands! I need three hands to make dinner. I only have two. Hey!"

"Hey what?"

"There's a hummingbird right there outside the window."

"At the feeder?"

"Yeah. Where did he go?"

I continued to peel potatoes. "Maybe he had other things to do."

"Maybe he went home. Or! Maybe he went to a tiny Costco for tiny snacks."

I shook my head. *The silliest things.*

One of the things I liked about living with Shelta and Crosby was the way we gathered around the dining table each evening. As soon as the food was before us, we took each other's hands and Shelta asked a blessing. I held Ryker's hand.

"So, yeah, this is good."

"Why, thank you, Ryker. I guess sausage and potatoes aren't so bad."

He picked up a couple of buttery potatoes that I had sliced in the shape of french-fries and popped them into his mouth. "Yeah, really good."

Shelta scolded Ryker, "Don't talk with your mouth full." Then she said to me, "How did you do this? They're amazing."

"Butter." I smiled. "Lots of butter."

"Well, I guess that's okay once in a while."

Hogan looked over my left shoulder. "So, how are you doing, my two new daughters? Do you like it here?"

I did like it here, but there were so many trains of thought going through my head, like, *what now? Is this your life plan?* I answered diplomatically, "Does anyone not like it here?"

Crosby looked pleased.

I heard knocking.

Shelta asked, "Ryker, are you knocking on the table?"

Ryker grinned mischievously, continued steadily knocking under the table. "No, I'm knocking on my head."

I asked him, "Is anybody home?"

"Nope."

Shelta laughed. "You're a good egg, Ryker"

He grinned. "Then you're a good hen."

CHAPTER TWELVE

Drake Friendship

"Great day for a brisk walk, right?"

The clean fragrance of Drake mingled with the seaspray and warm spice of cypress in the morning sun. "Hi Drake, is this a hawkeye day?"

"Indeed. Today, hawkeye at work. Where's Uny? Shall we all take a walk to the seals?"

"She's at a mid-morning yoga class with Crosby."

"Then shall we? If someone loves a place as much as I love this shoreline, he likes to show it off. I don't want to miss a fresh opportunity to give credit to God for this gorgeous scenery." He waved an arm in an arc as if to present the view. "Do you need to get permission to leave?"

"No. I'll just tell Ivy." I tilted my head toward the ocean-front office.

A canopy of cypress shaded the walkway along the first section of our path to produce a deep green pool from the gray Pacific water in the bay. "Hey Drake, did you notice that your legs are a bit longer than mine?"

The crows on the branches seemed to think that was funny as they chuckled along with Drake. "Sorry. I'll slow down."

I could barely hear him above the morning cacophony of seabirds surrounding the seal maternity ward beach.

"So Grace, what is it now? A month? How are you doing? Both of you. How is Uny doing?"

"It's hard to believe, but it is getting close to a month. There are so many things that are great, both for Uny and for me. Thanks for asking. We are both homesick though. Uny says so a lot."

"Did you both have a lot of friends where you came from?"

I smiled. "Yes, Uny has a lot of friends wherever she goes." I paused to watch a mamai seal inch her blob body onto the sand from the water then rumble her way to her pup. "So cute. So cute. I didn't have a lot of friends, only one very good one who I was just getting to know before we left home." I felt my cheeks heating up.

"A guy? A boyfriend?"

"Sort of. We didn't know each other very well yet. His name is Zane."

"And you left home and Zane to come to live with your Cousin Shelta?"

"Yes. It's complicated" I felt a deep pain somewhere between my left lung and my heart. I looked up at Drake. "Texas. We came from Texas."

He accepted my diversion willingly. "Really? I wouldn't have guessed Texas! So what did you do with most of your time in the Lone Star State?"

I answered his second question first. "I'm an aspiring writer."

Drake shook his head. "I've always found it hard to write."

"When I tell people, a lot of them say that. It is hard work, that's true, but it's weird how I like doing it. What's even weirder; I'll tell you something I've never told anyone. I think God has called me to write. Does that sound crazy to you?"

"No. Why would that sound crazy? Jesus told His believers that they were the light of the world and that they shouldn't hide their light under a basket. Writing must be the way He wants you to light your candle."

I stared up into those clear blue eyes for a moment. "Wow, Drake! That really helps me with my biggest challenge. I'm lacking the confidence that when I'm ready to put something out there, it will be poorly received. What I write could be terrible. It seems like that would be the worst thing, but it would be worse if I were too afraid to try."

We studied the seals, sand, and water for a moment before I switched back to our former subject. "We've only lived in Texas for a few years, that's why there's no drawl, y'all."

Drake smiled.

I smiled back and continued, "Actually, that's the longest we've lived anywhere. Our accent is derivative Irish. We're Irish American Travelers. Some call us gypsies."

He nodded. "So yeah. Irish. I thought that's what I've been hearing from Shelta and Crosby, but I didn't know for sure. Could've been Scottish for all I knew. My family came from New York originally but moved to LA when I was young. I've been hearing a melting pot of accents all my life. I should have probably paid more attention to their origins. Many of them were right in my own house." He studied the waves beyond the rocks momentarily, then continued. "You look perplexed."

"I am. What do you mean right in your own house but don't know the origin of them?"

He grinned. "My father was an actor."

"Would I have seen him in anything?"

"Probably, but I doubt you'd remember him. He worked mostly off-Broadway in New York for a while before we came to Hollywood so he could audition for a major part in a TV show." He paused as if recalling the past then shook his head slightly. "He didn't get the part. Ended up with the bit parts you wouldn't remember him in and lots of unemployment." He turned to face me, leaning against the temporary fence that reinforced the railing. "So mostly, he's in my memories alone and not as an actor but as a tinker."

"So, he's gone?"

"Yes. He died about nine years ago from lung cancer. He never got to meet my daughter, Lily. He loved to make things and fix things. Good with tools. Thanks to the long stretches of unemployment, I got to spend a lot of time with him and found I was also good with my hands. I was also artistic." Beneath his bronzed skin, he was blushing.

"Was?"

"When I was in high school, I majored in art and got a full-ride scholarship to a university, but I blew it off and traveled up the coast to Canada with a friend and then continued on my own to Cape Cod to visit one of my brothers."

"Brothers? Cape Cod? That's in the far Northeast, right?"

"Not that far from New York, actually. Both of my parents were married before. I have two half-sisters and two half-brothers in the New York area. When I returned to LA, I got a construction job with a general contractor, who took me under his wing. He let me observe and helped me learn.

He encouraged me to ask the subcontractors lots of questions."

"Look! Was that a whale? I thought I saw a spray go straight up."

"I didn't see it. Oh! There it is arching. Did you see that?"

"I did!" We kept our eyes glued to that spot upon the water. "So your mother supported you and your father?"

"Pretty much. She had a steady job at a popular restaurant and she was popular too. She brought home more in tips than she did in salary."

"How did you end up in Northern California?"

"I had a second job in LA as a bartender. The bar chain needed a manager on Cannery Row." He tilted his head toward the well-walked street a mile away. That's where I met my wife, Paige. She was a waitress at the Sardine Factory. That's also where she met Whelan, her husband now."

"Oh, I'm sorry. And you have a daughter? How old is she?"

"She just turned seven." His eyes were filled with turmoil and sadness.

I looked at the fading line on his left hand. "It wasn't all that long ago was it?"

"Actually, it's been a while, but I just recently took off my ring."

"Symbolic maybe? Are you ready to move on?"

"Not really. I kept wearing the ring because I was sure Paige will be the only wife for me. I still believe that. I suppose also I left the ring on as I sort of cruised along without a plan. I often feel as if most of us have no idea what we're doing, but we keep living life anyway. I'm different now though. I've changed. My wedding ring began to remind me of my former life and my failures."

I pondered his candor and chose to respect it with silence. The tumbling green silver of the water whispered to us with suck and pull, punctuated by a barking pup and squealing gulls on the rock beyond the seal's beach. It seemed a lot of words were resting uncomfortably between us, wanting to be spoken.

"I saw an ad for the handyman job at the Seal Harbor Inn."

"So that's how you ended up here."

"Yes. Here and also at Munras Grace in Monterey."

I jerked to look at him. "Munras Grace? That's the church where Uny I went to for help when we arrived here on a bus. We needed an angel."

"And you found Tina, right?"

I felt my eyes go wide. "How did you know?"

"She's the one that hired me to be *their* handyman. She *is* an angel. A real one. Do you know what angel means?"

"Um. No, I guess I never thought about it."

"Messenger of God. She was the messenger that introduced me to my Savior, Who is the reason why my life has changed."

CHAPTER THIRTEEN

Emails with Josie

Josie to Grace:

Wow! Of course, you didn't want to marry Zane's pa! Gosh, gypsies. Where were you coming from when I met you? Is your family still on the road? Sounds like not, unless that home you'd be living in with Zane and his father was on wheels. Tell me about Zane, please. How did you get to know him? How's Uny?

Grace to Josie:

So you asked me about Zane, and I could just say the most important thing about him: He's got a strong faith in God. He's not extremely handsome, but I really like his face. He's kind. He's a hard-working mechanic specializing in imported cars. He's a musician and a poet. But, the answer to "how did I get to know him" is a lot more revealing. Our families have been friends forever, I was betrothed to Zane's brother, Collen, for a couple of years, but Collen died. Zane gave me a flower at Collen's funeral then he brought me another flower every time he came to see me at my home after that.

Uny is good, but she seems restless. I keep wondering if I made a huge mistake bringing her here, but I'd hate to think about what a mistake it may have been not to.

I have a new friend here. His name is Drake. Just friends, really, even though he certainly is good looking. He's the handyman here at the motel. He also has a strong but new faith. He's quite a bit older than Uny and I. I don't know why I feel this way, but it seems as if God sent us to Drake so he could encourage and protect us.

So how's everything going? Have you made any new friends?

Josie to Grace:

I'm good still. Really good. Much better than I have been these past few years. I still love being here with Dad and Kris, and my counselor is helping me a lot. I'm beginning to believe that the things that happened to me were not my fault. Not that all my fears, imaginations, and feelings of shame are gone; they definitely are not. Mostly, I still get nightmares, but sometimes daymares too. I'm finding a lot of comfort reading the Bible.

For someone so young, you sure have been through a lot already! Engaged. Fiancé Died. In love with his brother. Moved to the ocean in California. Met a new "friend." Are you even 21 yet?

CHAPTER FOURTEEN

Shelta

Grace and Uny's arrival made Shelta happy. Not only because she was happy to be their escape route from weird traditions but for several other reasons. She enjoyed their company. It was great to have the household help from Grace, a friend for Ryker, and in a lesser degree, also to have Grace and Uny available as motel employees. Primarily, it made Shelta happy because her husband, Hogan Crosby, who was an axiomatic Dr. Jekyll and Mr. Hyde, was more likely to play his part as the kind doctor when other people were around.

Regardless of her awkward situation as a single woman expecting a baby, if Shelta had known six years ago the truth about Hogan's volatile personality, she would not have married him. At thirty, she married a widower twenty-seven years her senior. He rescued her from unwed-mother humiliation and a life of financial struggle as a single parent, but his belligerent moodiness was unworthy of the tradeoff. She had been attracted to his strength and the challenges of helping him with the remaining children at home, a few teenagers ready to fly the nest. Unlike many of the Travelers who kept several generations under their roofs or traveling caravan care, Crosby encouraged his sons to start their own lives. He did his best to arrange for his daughters to marry into good families. Since Shelta was already friends with several of his grown children, she felt at the time that the arranged match with Crosby was good, and she had thanked her pa. It was a perk that Hogan was going into business for himself, seventeen hundred miles away from the Travelers' usual circuits. However, before they married, Shelta saw only Hogan's sanguine side.

The first time her husband threw one of his now routine temper tantrums, Shelta was shocked. Thinking back, she couldn't remember what triggered it, and for that matter, since that time she could rarely analyze what could have possibly triggered any of them. Deep bouts of remorse followed, accompanied by pleas for punishment or for-giveness. It was craziness, as if what he wanted was for her to hate him because he thought he deserved it. Afterward, he would turn around and blame her for his violent outbursts. Many of these tantrums were followed by over-the-top benevolent acts, like a delivery of fifty long-stemmed roses. What she knew for sure was, in spite of this passive aggression, she was not his trigger. Raised in a home with four brothers instilled in her the confidence normally only bestowed upon the Traveler men. It was ironic to her that she married someone who liked to hang out with women because Shelta had always felt more comfortable being one of the boys.

She sought help from a counselor and learned methods to manage Hogan's spells of instability, but there seemed to be no way to stop them. There had to be underlying emotional problems triggering his intermittent fury. She tried to talk him into coming with her to the counselor, but he refused. She decided to tolerate his angry moods and leverage the counselor's tools, plus the Bible tool that seemed to help the most: "A gentle answer turns away wrath." Leaving Hogan was not an option because she loved the business and he was good to Ryker. If the latter were not true, even though managing Seal Harbor was the most fulfilling thing she had ever experienced, she would have separated from Hogan. She didn't *love* managing the motel more than she loved Ryker, but it was more satisfying. She felt more confident to run a business than she did to parent with the wisdom and knowledge she was going to need to help a little boy turn into a successful adult.

Against Catholic standards, when Ryker was born, Shelta asked her gynecologist to tie her fallopian tubes. Hogan didn't care. He said he had enough kids and had no desire to go to confession so he could take communion. Shelta had noticed his abstinence from both of those Catholic institutions long before Ryker's birth and her tubal ligation. When she suggested that they switch entirely to a Protestant church, Hogan was more apathetic than compliant. After several Sundays visiting new places, they landed at a non-denominational Bible church. Shelta felt at home. The people seemed sincerely welcoming, and she loved the music. Primarily, she was delighted with the preschool, middle school, and youth programs for Ryker. Hogan liked it too, confessing to her that he'd long felt oppressed by the traditions and rituals of their ancestors. More importantly, on their first Sunday, he ran into several of his female fitness buddies.

CHAPTER FIFTEEN

Uny on the Loose

Loosey, the baby seal, wasn't the only nipper on the loose. Shelta only needed us to work a few days each week, but although she merely paid us minimum wage, she didn't subtract our room and board. I occupied most of my spare time helping with the household and hanging out with the totally adorable Ryker. Uny, on the other hand, had a pocketful of money and an abundance of idle time. She started disappearing for a few hours at a time and then for full days, barely making it home in time for dinner.

"So where did you go today, Uny?"

She smiled at the rest of us around the table. "I have some new friends."

"Of course you do," I quipped. I turned to Shelta. "Uny makes friends easily."

Shelta rolled her eyes and looked at Crosby. "We can tell."

He looked over Uny's left shoulder and grinned. "I make friends easily too."

"Sure you do as long as they are women."

He looked over Shelta's left shoulder and shrugged. "Yes. I suppose that's true."

"Tell us about your new friends, Uny."

"Josh, Felicia, and Dave work at Bubba Gump's. Dave's girlfriend works at The Fish Hopper. Anna works at one of the gift shops next to Bubba's. They hang out together at Bubba Gump's a lot, usually when one of the three is working but sometimes when they're not."

It seemed innocent enough, until—one night Uny wasn't home in time for dinner. I called her mobile phone at least five times. It went immediately to voicemail. I felt a surge of hope when I remembered I'd installed a tracking app on her phone, but when I accessed it, there was no response. We ate without her in uncomfortable silence except for a few witticisms from Ryker. He was more content than I was when we answered, "We don't know," to his question, "Where's Uny?"

We washed up the dishes, tried calling her too many times to count, and were frantically worried by seven thirty. I pulled off my apron. "I'm going down to Bubba Gump's to see if I can track her down. I remember the names, Dave and Josh. Do you remember any others?"

Shelta looked up to the ceiling as if she would find answers written there. "Just Felicia."

Crosby looked distraught. "I'll go with you."

"Hogan, how about I call Drake and see if he can go with Grace? I'm thinking you might be too much of a father figure for anyone to open up to."

"Well I am and I want to protect her."

"Of course you do, but we need to find her and you may scare people into silence."

Bubba Gump's was packed. First, Drake scanned the bar section to see if she was there, thinking that although she was only eighteen, she would be allowed to sit within that area because of food service. It was loud, so I yelled to Drake, "Where do we start? Who do we ask?"

Drake took my hand and wove us back through the bar crowd to the restaurant's host pedestal. He cut in front of the first couple in line, put his palm up facing them. "Sorry. We won't try to take your table. This is an emergency."

Drake leaned in toward the host, "We need to talk to the manager."

The host, whose nametag read "Trevor" looked directly at me. I saw recognition cross his face. He asked, "Are you sure you need the manager? May I help you with something?"

"You've seen me here before, right?"

"Well, er, I thought so, but—"

Drake moved close to his face and quietly uttered, "Listen, Trevor, her sister is missing and I think you know who she's with. Get the manager and tell him or her that we need to talk to or find three of your employees right now, unless you'd rather we call the cops."

"Um, okay." Trevor's motions were twitchy as he pinched a microphone on his lapel, spoke into it then looked directly into Drake's eyes. "She'll be right here. Can I please seat these people?"

We stepped aside.

Trevor looked at the map on his pedestal, spoke into his microphone again. A waiter came up behind him, took some menus, and led the first couple in line toward the tables by the bay.

A tall, dark-haired woman came up to Trevor. He spoke to her for a moment and then pointed to us.

"Hi. I'm Amanda, the manager tonight. I understand you want to talk to three of our employees?"

Drake put out his hand, "Hi Amanda, this is Grace. I'm Drake."

She shook his hand. She gazed up into his handsome face, looking as if she wouldn't mind hanging on to that large grip a bit longer nor would she have minded if I were not there.

"Grace's sister is missing. We understand that she's been hanging out here with Josh, Dave, and Felicia. Are any of them here tonight?"

"Oh dear. This is not good."

"Why is that?"

"I'm only one of the assistant managers, but I heard that our boss let Josh go a few days ago. I've never heard of Dave or Felicia though. We used to have a David that worked here a few years ago, but..."

"Do you know why Josh was fired?"

Anxiety crossed Amanda's face, "Drugs."

"He used drugs while he was working?"

"Sold them, I think."

I put my hand over my heart. I felt my knees buckle.

Drake wrapped his arm around me and held me upright. He asked Amanda, "Can we please have Josh's address."

"I'm sorry, I don't have access to employee records and I'm not sure I could give that to you if I did. But maybe if you come back tomorrow after ten, the general manager will give it to you."

Drake stared at her a moment. "Thank you. What's the general manager's name?" With his arm still wrapped around me, Drake had to feel my confidence deflate along with my trembling, emotional breath. He patted the outside of my arm. "It's going to be okay."

"Yang. Edgar Yang."

Drake asked if I was okay before he released me and turned me to walk in front of him. His hands held the outside of both of my arms as he steered me between the line of people at Trevor's podium and the wall. I felt him stop, release me and turn around. Trevor had tapped Drake on the shoulder. He pressed a note into Drake's hand. Drake looked at the note and extended his hand. "Thanks, Trevor."

I asked, "What's that?"

"Josh's address. I know where this is."

An alley-like driveway separated the tiny house from the house next door. The two houses shared a garage with two single-car doors. When Drake knocked, we heard a deep voice grumbling then stillness. Drake knocked again. There were thumping noises then more silence.

Drake motioned to me to stay where I was. When he reached the side of the house toward the driveway, a red Camaro rolled passed Drake and angled into the street. Tires squealed. A wake of acrid tire smoke trailed the car. When I turned from watching the escape, Drake had disappeared. Seconds later, the door opened in front of me. Drake's voice trembled, "You'll need to be the one—she's in the bedroom."

"Oh, Uny! Oh, honey!" First, I covered her naked body, then I fell next to her onto the smelly bed to hug her and cry.

She moved and moaned softly, "Gracie?"

"Yes. Sweetheart. Grace is here. Drake is with me. He's waiting for us in the living room." I rolled off the bed, stood up, wiped my eyes and nose on the sleeve of my hoody jacket, and assessed the room. I was standing on Uny's clothes. "Come on, Uny. Wake up. We need to get you out of here." I sat back down on the bed, pulled her up beside me and helped her dress, all the while sickened, stunned, and acutely aware of the stain behind us, the evidence of Uny's lost virginity.

CHAPTER SIXTEEN

Drake Bishop

"Don't argue, Uny. We're taking you to the hospital, and we're going to ask for a rape kit." Drake kept his eyes on the road but rocked his head from side to side several times to relieve the tension that had climbed up into his shoulders and neck. He felt protective of these girls.

Uny whined softly, "No, Drake. He didn't rape me. I didn't know we were going to um—, but I wanted to go to his house. It's my fault."

This incident with Uny was like a punch in the gut. It brought home his biggest nightmare; his fear that at some future day, something like this could happen to Lily. His friend, Mark, accused him of giving full custody to Paige and Whelan because Drake wanted minimal child support, but Mark was wrong. Drake had more confidence that Whelan Becker, with his gated home in Carmel and his substantial wealth, would offer Lily greater opportunities and security than Drake ever could. He was relieved when he made the decision to give them full custody, but he was also sick about it. He loved Lily with a deep love that began the instant he held her for the first time on the day she was born. When they handed him the tiny, wrapped bundle, he knew his life would have to change to deserve this. How could he feel so much love for someone who didn't exist yesterday?

He also still loved Paige but knew he deserved neither of them. Whelan treated Paige and Lily well, not only financially. He was a good guy. But the lack of safety and privacy that Lily would be exposed to if she lived part-time with Drake in his tiny apartment was not the half of it. Drake was determined he would never be sucked back into drugs or even associate with his former crowd, but he was unable to forgive himself for the failures that destroyed his marriage and nearly destroyed his life. Now, his newly found faith empowered him to choose, moment by moment, to live victoriously. But, he longed for a day when unexplainable peace would prevail, the day when memories could surface without the agony of regret.

In his rearview mirror, Drake saw Grace squeeze her sobbing sister's shoulders. "Drake's right, Uny. You're eighteen, so no one has to notify the police right away or anything but listen to him. Right now, you're humiliated, and you think it's your fault, but when you come out of this stupor, you may want the evidence. Unless—"

Uny mumbled into Grace's shoulder, "Unless what?"

"I don't suppose he used protection?"

Uny's sobbing intensified. "N-n-no."

"I'll stay by your side as much as possible at the hospital and I won't be far if they don't let me stay right there with you."

There was something about Grace. It was hard for Drake to believe that she was only twenty. She seemed to have powerful wisdom and energy about her that engaged people instantly. An ease and confidence within her seemed to pull the room toward her, as if she were its heart or center. He knew that, even in this horrible crisis, Grace was capable of comforting Uny and providing her with strength and wisdom to face tomorrow.

Drake growled, "I'm pretty sure the hospital will do a blood test and possibly a urine test, to see if that creep gave you any drugs to decrease your willpower. They'll probably want to keep your clothes for evidence." He added more gently, "Once I get the two of you settled into qualified medical hands, I'll go to Seal Harbor to tell Shelta and Crosby what happened in person and ask Shelta to find some clean clothes to send back with me."

Drake made a detour on the way to his car. He stepped off the verge of the hospital parking lot into a wooded area and heaved his guts at the base of a cypress tree. He returned to his car and pulled a small towel from his trunk. Careful to avoid the corner he had used to wipe his hands after adding engine oil, he wiped his face then leaned against the vehicle. His emotions were raw. He allowed himself the rarity of tears then wiped his face again before descending to his seat behind the wheel. He slid his phone from his pocket. "Hi, Paige. Yeah, I'm okay. Sorry to call so late. Yeah, everything's okay, well, no. Something's happened to a friend of mine, one of the girls I told you about who are staying with Shelta at Seal Harbor. She's going to be okay, but all of this made me miss Lily. Is she still up? May I say goodnight?"

When he heard his daughter's voice, he replied, "Hi, sweetheart. I just called to say night-night. I'm blowing a hug and kisses all the way to Carmel. Are they there yet? Wow. Yup, I got yours. What a mighty hug! I love you, sweetie. When you pray, please pray for Daddy. I'll pray for you too. Ni-night.

"Thanks, Paige. I needed that. Yes." He paused. "How'd you guess? You're so intuitive, as always. Yeah, Uny, the younger one. She's got a wild side coupled with naivety.

That's what I was thinking too, but I guess it was somewhat consensual, I think, but I'm not sure. Thanks. She doesn't know you, but she needs all the prayers she can get. I sure hope the kid isn't pregnant. Yeah, well, apparently, he didn't. Okay. Now I gotta go tell Shelta and Crosby. Say 'hey' to Whelan for me."

CHAPTER SEVENTEEN

Recuperation

I plugged Uny's totally dead mobile phone into the charger. I sarcastically accused the futility of the situation. *Lot of good it was to put the Family and Friends GPS Tracker on a phone that someone forgot to charge. Who would have thought something we installed to help find a lost phone would be crucial to find a lost sister?* I changed the conversation with myself in my head from what was now in the past to what needed to be done. *Of course, I'll have to tell Mamai about Uny as soon as I can. My courage seems to have flown away. I need to plan my words. I'll leave a message, and then when Mamai calls back, I'll need to be positive and encouraging. She was so strong and decisive when she helped us leave, but I'm worried about her. Every time I think about Mamai I feel a little twinge in my gut. I'm afraid this will be too much for her. Her mind might slip over the edge of sanity.* I busied myself in the oceanfront office as I noodled what to say and how to say it. I dusted the racks, swept the floor, wiped the counters, and checked the coffee level. I restocked brochures and newspapers. I had one foot out on the deck before I spun around on one heel and walked back to the newspaper rack. A small text box below the *Monterey Pine* masthead read, "Mystery Poet Submits

Again—Page 3." I hurriedly tucked a copy of the paper into my cleaning caddy and shot out the door in search of a private place to read page three. I collided with a man.

"Oh! I'm so sorry sir. Are you okay?" *Do I know him?*

"I'm fine. I'd be pretty fragile if someone as tiny as you could hurt me." He regarded me with dark eyes that devoured me with curiosity. He had an open, handsome face and his teeth flashed as he laughed.

I felt the heat rise in my neck.

"You must be Grace. I'm Burne. Burne Crosby. Hogan's seventh son of the seven sons before Ryker."

My first quick impression of Burne Crosby was that he wore a mask of controlled humor to hide some strong emotion, as if he was mocking life. He looked a little older than I was. Probably one of the teenagers still at home when Shelta married Crosby. "Oh, I thought you looked familiar. It must be because you look like your pa."

He straightened his shoulders and smoothed back his hair in a gesture I was to know well. "Only with dark hair and a goatee beard, right? Some people mistake me for Johnny Depp."

"Oh," I repeated, aware of my limited vocabulary. "Um, yeah, and then there's that. I wondered whose beautiful car that was that's parked next to Shelta's Cadillac in their carport."

"Pa lets me move the Jeep out and put my Beemer under the carport when I come to stay." He had the slightest Irish lilt, which I found charming. Even without the accent, there was no doubt about this man's ancestry. He was classic black Irish. Dark wavy hair, deep, almost black brown eyes, and olive complexion. He wasn't tall and though he was slenderly built, he had a strength in him that told you he would be an ugly customer in a fight, accompanied by a readiness to find an excuse to join one.

"Will you be staying long?"

"Not sure yet." His frank, appraising eyes met mine. "I have some business to take care of. I'm not sure how long it'll take. Maybe a week." His eyes scrutinized my face. "Maybe longer now."

I felt the heat of a full-on blush. I looked at my caddy and the newspaper. "Well, I'm sure I'll see you again. I should get on with my work."

"See you at dinner."

I knew the poem was Zane's.

Miss my miss

   Uneven are my thoughts

   Unrestful is my sleep

   Unsteadily beats my heart

Here without you.

   Will not surrender to lost hope

   Cannot ask the one who knows

I must come to you, but where?

I ran my fingers over each line as if I could touch him seventeen hundred miles away. *My miss.* I loved that. At that moment, I missed him awfully like someone who had died. The nagging thoughts and guilt rose within me yet again. *What have I done? What could I have done instead?*

The article mentioned it was the third poem, so I typed the newspaper's web address into my phone and indeed, there were archived articles. I heard footsteps on the deck outside the door of the room I was supposedly cleaning. I shoved the phone back into my pocket and the newspaper back into my caddy.

"Grace?"

I stepped out from my hiding place behind the bathroom door. "Uny! You're up." I wrapped my arms around my sister. "You smell good." I smiled as I backed up from our hug. Did you have a nice shower?"

"Yeah. I stayed in so long, I was afraid the Inn would run out of hot water."

"How are you feeling?"

"Still tired, but I can't stay in bed forever. I want to, but I can't. As you've been reminding me, my life needs to go on, and I can start making good choices going forward. I'll need to be out of bed to make choices." Her eyes glistened. Her hands were trembling as she pulled the damp hair aside that had fallen in her face.

"Oh, Uny. I'm so proud of you. Have you had anything to eat?"

"Just the tea and toast you brought me this morning."

"Come on, I'll take lunch now. I made some of my Extraordinary Chicken Salad this morning."

"Oh yum! Did you make your almonds too, or are we using shoestring French fries this time?"

"I toasted some almond slivers in butter."

"That helps me feel hungry. Hey, Grace, do celebrities hang out around here?"

"The only one I've heard of is Clint Eastwood, Why?"

"I thought I just saw Johnny Depp."

"No, I know, right? It's not. Trust me. Far from it. It's Hogan's son, Burne, and he's way younger than Johnny Depp. I have something else to tell you too." I flicked the newspaper. "Look. A mystery poet has been sending messages to the local newspaper."

Her eyes went wide. "Zane?"

I grinned. "I'm sure it is. Let's call Mamai and leave a message. I'll tell you the little I know about Burne while we eat lunch and wait for her to call back. I want us both to leave the message. I know it's corny, but I want her to hear your voice before we break the news about your, um, I want to call it an abduction."

"But it was not. It was a stupiduction."

CHAPTER EIGHTEEN

Almost Persuaded

Mamai's call to my phone ended our lunch at the kitchen table. Considerately as possible, I told her Uny's story. Mamai was so upset, I doubted her ability to recover emotionally and to continue her masquerade. Would she be unable to add this tragic news of Uny's indiscretion to her other secrets from Pa? I handed my phone to Uny and paced the kitchen, listening to Uny's side of the conversation.

Mamai had gone out for a walk to call us. I prayed Mamai's lengthy conversation in the blistering, Texas sun wouldn't cause her to have a heat stroke. Uny cried the entire time and Mamai sounded nasally when it was my turn to talk to her again. Mamai asked the same questions over and over, repeated my replies back to me, and then repeated her own answers too. It was as if her mind could process neither our news nor her own thoughts. I didn't count how many times we used it, but between the three of us, we may have worn out the word "sorry." Before we hung up, in a shaky voice, Mamai pleaded, "Please send a text to this phone the minute Uny starts her period. If she doesn't, you know we'll have to reconsider everything."

After I tapped to end the call, I said, "You look exhausted, Uny."

"This is only the beginning. I'm gonna pay for my stupidity for a long time, aren't I?"

"Probably. But right now, why don't you go lie down before dinner? I'll go finish my day. Drake brought by a few novels. Did you see them? I set them down next to the Bible the church gave you. His ex-wife loaned them to us. She told him to tell you they were wholesome, positive, and inspirational. And they have great stories. Why don't you get lost in someone else's story for a little while? Later, we can go for a walk to visit the baby seals."

"Drake has an ex-wife?"

"Yes. Her name is Paige. He has a daughter named Lily."

"Oh my, I feel sad for him, but happy too because he has a daughter. I should get to know him better. Everyone has their own story, don't they?"

"Indeed they do. I'm hoping to write some of those stories. I wish I hadn't lost my notebook on the bus."

"My beautiful Gracie. Everything is preserved in the nooks of your brilliant mind. Like you tell me all the time: Look at the positive side. The content of your notebook was stolen, not lost."

"Yes, I suppose that's true, but in this case, I feel like some things are lost. I wrote about Anna and Hannah and Josie."

"Those stories are not totally gone. Write about them tonight and tomorrow night and the next night."

"I will. Thank you. I remember some of the other things I wrote. I'll try to recreate some of my feelings."

"About Zane?"

"Yes, but there was a lot there. Uny, this is good. Your concern for Drake and his family and encouraging me to return to writing. I'm proud of you. It's a sign of maturity to be thinking of others and to have compassion, especially with your own story singing its song so loudly in your head. Please go rest. I need to get back to work, but it will only take a few minutes to wash up our lunch dishes."

Uny said, "Thank you," and then took her hot, swollen face and eyes to our room.

I turned back to the sink. Burne was leaning within the kitchen doorframe. I had not heard him arrive. "Oh, Hi, Burne."

"Hello. So that's your sister. You look a lot alike." He raised one eyebrow. "But you are definitely the most beautiful."

I found his praise oddly moving and, once again, felt redness returning to my neck and cheeks. "Er, um, thank you." *Could I only speak in two-letter words around this man?*

"Here, hand me that towel. I'll dry those and put them away. I heard you tell your sister that you need to get back to work."

I was flustered. For some reason, I didn't want him to be so nice to me and I felt the need to flee. And yet, I did not want to part from him. I felt the warmth of his hand as we passed the thin dishtowel. His eyes were like agates. "Well, okay thank you. Yeah. I'll get back to work." I turned and sketched a wave from the kitchen door. "See you later."

From the second story deck of the ocean-front rooms, trying to regain my sense of peace, I prayed without words or definable thoughts. I merely turned all meditations to the Creator as I paused to delight myself in the surf and waves that He set in motion. I pondered His words to Job I had read the other day and was humbled.

"Who shut up the sea behind doors

when it burst forth from the womb,

when I made the clouds its garment

and wrapped it in thick darkness,

when I fixed limits for it

and set its doors and bars in place,

when I said, 'This far you may come and no farther;

here is where your proud waves halt?"

I set aside my fears for Uny and Mamai, my longing for home and Zane, and the magnetic pull I felt toward Burne. I allowed the tide that sucked and swirled among the rocks to work its therapeutic magic in my soul. The morning clouds had given way to brilliant sunshine. The bay looked different from my second story vantage point. High, clear light poured into it. There had been a little snap of storm during the night with strong winds that died with the dawn, but it had freshened the needles on the cypress trees, washed the lattice fence that separated the walking path from the few seals who had lumbered onto the small beach below, and cleaned the road in front of the Inn. The sand was dazzling in the sun and the echo of the storm had turned the usual ripple on the bay's edge into three-foot waves. I directed my attention to my work with renewed hope that everything would work out and that God would give me the strength to meet the future.

Having Burne at the dinner table drew a good mood from the ever-moody Crosby, and Burne lifted each of us up in other ways. He insisted Shelta and I have a night off. He purchased a fully-cooked dinner and picked it up from the

International Cuisine on Lighthouse Avenue. I had never tasted saffron rice. It was delicious. The rock cod from the Monterey Bay in Champagne caper sauce melted in my mouth. We tasted small cups of award-winning clam chowder. We melted butter onto warmed sourdough bread. There would be enough left over for tomorrow's lunch. Uny stole glances at him regularly. His handsome face and continual jokes kept her giggling. However, Burne directed most of his jokes toward Ryker, who hugged himself while laughing with each tease from his older brother.

"Does anyone want to split that last piece of fish with me?"

"Ah Burne," Crosby chuckled, "You haven't changed a bit." He turned to look somewhere between my left shoulder and Uny's right. "He would always do that. Never took the last piece of anything, even if he was in a squabble with his brother, Keely."

He grinned mischievously. "Ah yes. When we were kids, I loved to disagree with Keely."

Crosby laughed heartily. "Indeed, indeed, the most unusual and entertaining arguments, for both of you were sayin' the same thing and argued forcefully anyway." He laughed some more.

Uny asked, "What you do mean they were saying the same thing?"

"Oh, one time it was about prehistoric creatures. Keely insisted they were dinosaurs. Burne contested, 'No! They're T-Rexes.'"

Burne laughed. "Yes," he bobbed his head, "it's true. Guilty as charged." His head movement changed from little yeses to little nos, "Those were the days. God forbid that either of us would really listen to the other and accept that our opponent could be right."

I was more at home and relaxed at dinner than I'd been since we arrived in California. Burne had a semi-smile that seemed to be reserved for me. It lifted one side of his mouth, but mostly it drew me into his dark eyes. He talked with his hands, unlike his father who could not seem to look at anyone directly, Burne had a gregarious ability to make eye contact with each of us as he told us his stories. Often, as his eyes turned to me, he would lightly touch the top of my forearm. Ryker wasn't the only one to fall under his spell.

CHAPTER NINETEEN

Anita's First Crisis

Already fighting depression, Anita was overwhelmed by the news that Uny was date raped. A tornado of emotion, terrible and harsh, swirled and ached in her vital organs. She felt tired. Comatose tired. Wavering in a dizzy stupor she was aware she might fall from the bench where she had retreated to return Grace's call. This was the same bench on which she had handed her daughters all they needed to carry out the plan that ruined their lives. *Her* plan. She tried repeatedly to convince herself that it wasn't about her; her life was not ruined, and if it were ruined, releasing Grace and Uny from cult tyranny was the right thing to do. The tree positioned between her table and the sun was filled with a flock of incredibly noisy, chirping finches. The shadow of a thin branch moved and curtsied on the table as if it were her own confused and drifting thoughts. She resented the birds' obvious happiness. Anita tried to focus on the blessings of being the mother to her other two children, but none of the arguments she had with herself lifted her from self-focused misery. She felt constrained in every way. Her heart hurt, not just figuratively. It actually hurt in the left side of her breast each time she took a breath. Even before this devastating news, after she heard that the girls had lost everything on their bus trip, Anita had barely slept. On rare occasions, when she had finally drifted into an exhausted sleep, she would often jerk awake from terrifying dreams. Once, she woke after falling, falling, falling into a deep ravine. Another time, a freight train was heading directly toward her, but she woke before it hit. She was breathless, and her heart thumped against her breast. In her waking hours around the house, her mind tricked her into imaginary conversations with Grace or Uny. Most often it was Grace, who had always been beyond her years in maturity and wisdom. But then Anita would feel the stinging agony of reality, like a punch in her abdomen. Grace and Uny were not there. She would remember why and cry helplessly, as if there were neither love nor hope left in the world.

Cooey insisted that she go to a psychiatrist. Talking to Olivia, helped a little. Olivia was not allowed to tell anyone what Anita confessed. In fact, Anita was unsure if Olivia had any purpose at all except to listen. Nothing, not even the drugs Olivia prescribed, could help Anita absorb the news that her virgin daughter had been raped. Things that "only happened to other people" were happening to them, to her, to her precious Uny.

CHAPTER TWENTY

An Invitation

We were relieved that Uny seemed happy for the first time since her trauma. Everyone at the dinner table was enjoying her excitement over the baby seal. "When I couldn't find Loosey on the beach, I ran down to the big beach by the Aquarium and found Charlie. He told us they took her to the Marine Mammal Center yesterday."

Shelta and I were smiling. It had been too long since we'd seen her so perky.

Burne asked, "So you named a seal pup?"

Uny bubbled over, telling him the entire story of how we spotted her, met Charlie from Fish and Wildlife, why she had named the seal Loosey, and that she had been worrying and checking up on Loosey almost every day. She explained to Burne, "They have to be very careful rescuing babies. Charlie told us that interfering can cause other birthing mamais on that beach to miscarry."

Ryker, who had gone with us several times, clapped his hands. "Yay! No more Loosey on the loose!" He got up from his chair and continued a little marching dance until he successfully got us all chuckling.

Except for Crosby. He was in a bad temper.

Shelta looked weary. "Okay, okay, time to quit marching. Time to eat this delicious, casserole that Grace made for us." She turned to me. "Where did you get this recipe?"

"I call it Peter's casserole. Our neighbor back home, Margaret, who is a fabulous home-style cook, made it up. Her son, Peter, was sitting on the couch one day musing, 'I'm thinking ground beef, broccoli, Tater Tots, with melted cheese on top ...' Margaret went with that and added cauliflower."

Shelta finished chewing the bite in her mouth. "Mmmm. How come everything you make tastes so good?"

I spoke in my best Texas drawl, "Comfort food from the South, ma'am. As long as I'm here, I'll do everything I can to keep y'all comfortable." I deliberately avoided looking at Crosby as I thought to myself, *I don't know how she tolerates his changeable, irritable moods. Shelta deserves to have someone comfort her.*

Shelta patted her belly. "If I keep eating like this, my clothes won't be comfortable. Ryker! Your milk is overflowing. You need to stop blowing bubbles in your cup."

"I'm not going to stop. I'm the bubble master!"

"Yes. You certainly are the master, mister, but I want you to stop right now."

"How long are you girls here for?" asked Burne.

I stammered as I tried to answer. "Um. Well—"

Crosby interrupted, "They're here as long as they want to be," he looked directly over my left shoulder, "as long as you behave." He looked over Uny's shoulder.

A cynical, fleeting thought whispered, *I wonder if he is taking out employee life insurance policies on us.* "Thank you, Crosby."

Uny looked a little flustered at his comment about behaving. She spoke so softly I could barely hear her say, "Yes, thank you, Crosby."

I slid a bite of Peter's casserole onto my fork, I was thinking that Crosby had every right to expect us to behave, but I wished that he'd muster up some sensibility toward Uny's predicament and recognize her shame. I also wondered if Crosby had told Burne Uny's story.

I felt Burne watching me. The skin along the back of my neck prickled from the attention. "Well Grace, do you think you can behave if I take you out to dinner on Thursday?"

Shelta raised her eyebrows and smirked.

Uny's eyes got wide. She nudged me with her knee under the table.

Angry thought lines formed between Crosby's, dark, level brows as he looked over Burne's left shoulder.

My heart could've kept time with a hummingbird's wings. I replied as calmly as I could muster, "It's a date."

Ryker got up and started marching again, repeatedly singing. "It's a date," his hands and shoulders moved so wildly that his untrimmed hair slashed back-and-forth across his forehead.

CHAPTER TWENTY-ONE

The Worst Possible Consequence

"Uny, Honey. Are you okay?"

She was curled up in a fetal position on her bed. I could see smudges of sleepless terror under her eyes. "I'm late Grace. Should we buy a pregnancy test?"

I felt a little dizzy as the blood drained from my head. As shocked and saddened as I was, I didn't want to do or say anything that would upset her more than she already was, so I did my best to appear outwardly logical and steady. "Yes, we probably should." I zipped up my hoodie. "I'll ask Shelta if I can borrow the Jeep to go to CVS. Be right back." I gently closed the door of our room, but before I could approach Shelta, I braced myself with palms flat against our door. I was shaking all over with the numbing shock of grief. Wave after wave of apprehension fed upon my brain. I was angry with Uny's adversary. Inwardly I screamed at him, even swore at him, then I apologized to God and told Him I didn't want to think like that. I was certain He didn't want to hear my unspoken, nasty words. I took a deep breath, "I know, I know I need to forgive him. Don't know if I can do that yet, but I'll put it on my todo list, God; really I will. Right now I need to go to CVS." My palms were sweaty against the door as my whole body trembled uncontrollably. I fought my fears for Uny with the logic that, although this

120

might be a gigantic disruption in Uny's life and in the lives of all of us who loved her, I had a peaceful comforting thought, *A tiny life may have been introduced to this world.*

I wiped my sweaty palms on the front of my jacket, rubbed them together to bring back circulation, and went to the store for the test strip that would disclose if Uny was pregnant.

She was.

"Now what, Gracie?" She was back on her bed, sitting with her knees pulled up, rocking back and forth.

I felt tears wanting to spill from my eyes, but I did not permit them to have their way. I took a deep breath, prayed, and stated calmly, "The best way to forget how you feel is to concentrate on what you know for sure. Head above heart. Let logic rule. It seems to me there are only two logical paths, but several choices on each path."

"Two?"

"Yes. I guess there's only one thing to do, but two ways to go after that. You will have your baby, and then you will either keep it or give it to a loving family."

"I didn't think you meant abortion."

"No. I didn't consider that an option. Did you?"

"Well, I'd be lying if I said I didn't wish this never happened, and I didn't wish I could make it go away without everyone knowing. There will be so many consequences to my life for the next several months. I cringe thinking about major changes to my body. I mean I can understand how some women take that way out, but then again I can't really. To me, this is already my child, and I already love her. I want the best for her. Remember how happy I was when I found out Loosey was going to live at the Marine Mammal Center? I was happy because she was going to *live*. I should be at least as happy for my baby."

"To me, she is already your child too, Sweetheart. However, I'm not as sure as you are that she's a girl. You're so silly sometimes."

"That's putting it mildly."

I began to calm down. An innocent life deserved a loving welcome. As his or her aunt, I vowed to give that child as much love as was heavenly, not merely earthly possible. And Uny needed more love than ever. I was incapable to do this on my own. The hardest part was the first step: forgive the rapist. I needed to surrender all my selfish thoughts to the cross; crucify my fear, my anger, and other self-centered emotions that would block the flow of God's unconditional love from pouring through me to these two, whom God loves more than I do.

I sat down beside Uny, pulled my knees up as she had, and put my arm around her. We rocked together. "You're so brave, and I'm so proud of you. It's only nine months and one of those months is behind you. You'll only be visibly pregnant for about six months. That seems like a long time to feel your body change, get used to the idea of birth pains, and make all the necessary decisions, but I promise you, it won't seem too long. Gosh, it was nine months ago that Collen died. Seems like ages ago that I started seeing Zane."

She nodded. "Yeah, it does. On a planet far, far, away."

"Right? Living here by the cool ocean, it feels like Texas and ancient gypsy traditions are in another world. So Uny, you don't have to make up your mind right now about adoption or—"

"I already have."

"Really?"

"Yes. I want my baby to have a home with two parents who both want her. I don't want her to ask me about my stupid foolishness or wonder where her father is. And who knows where I'm going to end up? I may still end up back in our gypsy cult. I *really* don't want *that* for my baby, but I want to have a say about who she'll go to. I can do that, right? It happens that way on TV."

"Yes and we all know how everything we see on TV and the Internet is true. But, sarcasm aside, I'm pretty sure that *is* true. That's what I meant by several directions after you choose between keeping her or giving her up for adoption. I'm not sure if there is a name for it, like 'open adoption' or somesuch, but we can google it. If it's okay with you, I'll ask Shelta to help us?"

"Yes, please. Everyone is going to know soon enough anyway. Everyone."

"What do you mean?"

"Even though our insurance cards were stolen, we're still on Pa's insurance."

"Right. Our gypsy wanderings might be coming to an abrupt end unless we find another way to get you and your baby quality health care. Do you want to talk to Shelta yourself or do you want me to break the news?"

"And Crosby, please. Do you mind telling them without me?"

My timing was perfect. They were both home and Ryker was not. Burne had taken him to the Monterey Bay Aquarium, saying to Shelta that it didn't seem right to live so close and the kid rarely gets to go. He also wanted to go himself.

"Uny is pregnant."

They were silent. Silent? The air was fizzing as if there were small explosions in the air, like someone juggling Fourth of July sparklers.

Crosby muttered profanity then apologized for it. "They did a rape kit at the hospital, right? Tox screen, DNA?"

"Yes, but Uny doesn't want anything to do with him and is still too embarrassed to report it to the police. She blames herself."

I considered Shelta, whose eyes were damp and lumonous. She'd been here. I could almost hear her memories, fears, and sympathy in her silence. Finally, she uttered, "Poor kid."

Through the open window, the bay was noisy with crashing surf and the barking baby seals. A seagull's laughter mocked our silence as it flew past then faded away in a long, grieving cry.

"I suppose we need to go home. We're on Pa's health insurance."

For the first time since I had met him, instead of looking over my left shoulder, Crosby's eyes met mine. "That won't be necessary. I'll make arrangements for her prenatal care and pay for the delivery. Then all three of you are still welcome here."

I remembered what Mamai told us about Crosby's hatred of my father, and wondered if he knew how much this would hurt Pa if he found out. I was also overwhelmed by Crosby's generosity. I grabbed a tissue from Shelta's desk and wiped my eyes and nose. "Wow, Crosby. Thank you. Uny has time to change her mind, of course, but right now she says she's leaning toward giving her baby up for adoption."

CHAPTER TWENTY-TWO

Emails with Josie

Grace to Josie:

I'm so glad I have you to etalk to.

You asked me if I was 21 yet. No, not until next January.

You also referred to Zane as my love, but I'm not sure about that.

You haven't heard from me because I have to admit, I've been embarrassed on behalf of Uny and also on my own behalf. I keep thinking this wouldn't have happened if I had just stayed in Texas, surrendered to Pa and the cult customs, and married Zane's pa. Ew! The thought of that, though, still makes me feel sick to my stomach.

Uny was date raped. I've been feeling guilty for taking her away from our home. And I feel even guiltier because our mamai is not doing well at all. She seems to be losing her mind. I keep wondering if I should give up, go back, and quit trying to change the world.

And now, the worst has happened. Uny is pregnant. I haven't told Mamai yet. She knows about the rape, but not about the pregnancy. Please pray for us.

At first, I thought for sure we'd have to go back to the cult, but guess what? Shelta's husband, Hogan Crosby, offered to pay for Uny's health care and the cost of her having her baby! I was shocked when he offered but also grateful. So is Uny. She definitely didn't want to take her baby back to what we left behind. She wants to give her baby to a good family.

I have something else I'm embarrassed to tell you. After I told you I might be in love with Zane. I've accepted a date with someone else. He's Crosby's youngest son. His name is Burne. Well youngest in Crosby's first family. He has a six year old son, Ryker, Shelta's son. Burne is exceptionally handsome and seems to be enormously attracted to me. I get flustered by the attention he shows me. And, there's something he doesn't know. This will be my first date. I didn't date Collen. Zane and I never had an actual date. Zane did kiss me goodbye though. Oh gosh. What am I doing?

Sorry, I should have asked you first, how are you?

Josie to Grace:

Hi Grace!

I'm so sorry to hear about Uny. I'll keep praying for her, and your mom, and you. That's amazing how Crosby is stepping up to help. That's so generous of him!

So, a first date? How soon? How exciting! Did you make any promises to Zane? Did he make promises to you? Seems like you started on a new life and he would not expect you to stay attached to him. He probably wanted you to, but if he didn't ask you to, I don't know why you should feel guilty.

Tell me more about Burne. How old is he? What kind of work does he do?

I'm doing great. I don't know how much weight I've lost, but I feel really good. Kris told me I can weigh myself one day but not yet. She says healthy is the goal. The number on the scale will follow. I don't even like Pepsi anymore. Kris turned me onto sparkling water with no sugar.

CHAPTER TWENTY-THREE

Walking with Shelta

A low balustrade of pines, already smelling warm and spicy in the morning sun, hung over the sparkling bay. Shelta and I walked briskly along the beaten dirt walkway, leaving the adjacent strip of asphalt free for the bicycles and the two-person bicycle carriages, rented and ridden from Cannery Row. Since the first day of our arrival in Pacific Grove, my admiration for my cousin had increased daily as I observed her business acumen, her wisdom and kindness with Uny and me, her loving treatment of Ryker, and her gracious handling of the ever-moody Crosby. She seemed to watch rather than simply look at things as we took this early morning walk. I wondered how many intelligent, capable Irish Traveler women before her, including my exceptionally gifted mamai, had spent their entire uneducated lives, using all their talents to run households for men their fathers gave them to.

Shelta released a deep sigh. "Isn't this lovely? We didn't have to wait for clouds to lift this morning."

"It is lovely, and it's so wonderful to have time alone with you."

She paused, so I paused with her. "Aw. What a kind thing to say, Grace."

I asked boldly, "Are you lonely, Shelta?"

The corner of her mouth lifted slightly. "I suppose I am, or I was before you and Uny arrived."

"I wondered. I know you love your job and Ryker, but neither offers you adult companionship at a meaningful level. And then there's Crosby."

We began walking again.

"Yeah. And then there's Crosby." She said somewhat sardonically.

"The first night we were here, I heard him crashing things and yelling at you. Does that happen a lot?"

We stopped and looked over the railing at the corner of a frothy pool laced with seaweed. Gathering her open jacket to crisscross warmly across her breast as if in preparation to speak, she almost whispered, "Unfortunately, the answer is yes. I feel like my whole married life I've been trying to guess what will make him angry so I can steer clear of it. But it rarely works. I try to be so good he couldn't possibly get mad, but then he does anyway."

A curling wave broke and foamed the pool, then retreated withdrawing foam over damp sand at land's edge.

"Has he ever hurt you physically?"

"No, just verbally—lots of verbally—and emotionally, but there have been times when his anger frightened me, and I thought he might get physically violent too."

"Do you know how Aislyn died?"

She jerked her head from studying the shore and looked at me, "Yes. She had an accident. Fell down some stairs."

"Do you suppose it might not have been an accident?"

Two black crows began a noisy, nasty battle in the branches of the cypress above our heads. They squawked so loudly; we held our conversation until they took their combat out over the bay then circled back to the shore. One shouted angrily and chased the other inland until they were out of sight and hearing.

"That's a bit too familiar." She pulled the jacket close again to embrace herself. "I really don't think Crosby would murder the mother of his children intentionally, do you?"

"I think it's possible that in his anger he caused the accident." I paused. "And then he got away with it."

Shelta nodded as if she was pondering my words. "He sued the motel where she fell. Got a huge sum of money. Plus life insurance."

"Yes, of course. With the Travelers, there is always a hefty life insurance policy." I thought for a minute before asking, "Shelta, do you suppose he feels guilty for what happened to Aislyn and that's why he behaves so illogically and he is so cruel to you?"

She looked at me intently. "I've often wondered what it could be. I do his laundry, well okay, I pay Ivy to do his laundry, so I know he doesn't have burrs in his underpants."

"You're so funny."

We turned back toward the Inn and walked in silence, listening to the surf, the seagulls, the seals, and our thoughts. The barking got louder until we reached the beach belonging to the seals. A few of the pups waited impatiently for their mamais to return. The rest of the mamais and babies had bodies that were slack and contented. Some had closed their eyes, as if enjoying the morning sun. A fat, gray mermaid, waving her flippers gently, turned on her back to show us her pale, spotted stomach. Another came heaving out of the sea and flopped to where her pup lay. The baby stopped barking to nuzzle in and suck. Not very far from us, another baby lay quietly, apparently full and satisfied. Its big eyes stared at us with mild curiosity but without fear.

"Will you help me get ready for my date with Burne tonight?"

"Of course! Shall we go shopping?"

"Oh, could we? I'd love a new dress, and maybe can you help me pick out, and then later, put on makeup? Does this mean both you and I can desert Seal Harbor for a few hours today?"

"Yes we can. What's wrong, Grace? Are you afraid to go out with him?"

"Um, no, but kind of, yes. Actually, I wanted to talk to you." My words were a torrent of run-on sentences that I poured over Shelta with a release of pent-up emotion. First, I shared my fears because I'd never been on a date. I talked about my feelings, or lack of them, for Collen and the resulting guilt. And then told her everything, probably more than she wanted to hear about Zane and our running and rendezvous at the park, his few visits to our home, the flowers, the poem, the kiss, and the poems in the paper. "And now I feel like my date with Burne is a betrayal of Zane." I paused, to take a breath. "A betrayal, though Zane and I never had a date."

She listened carefully and let me spit out everything without interrupting. She had a way of doing that, warmly, even when she may have wanted to address something in my multifaceted paragraph. She had listened that way when I rambled on about Uny's crisis. I had observed her listen patiently to Ryker in the same manner. I felt so privileged to have had this opportunity to develop this friendship with my mamai's cousin, my cousin.

We scooted out of the sun into the shade of the cypress on the morning side of the path. This changed our immediate view from sandy blobs of seal bodies to a shingle carpeted with brilliant, white daisies, globular succulents, and hot pink ice plant. Bright, tangled flowers splashed down over sunlit rock.

"Are you in love with Zane?"

"I don't know. I thought it might be love, but can that be true? If I were in love with Zane, could I be this attracted to Burne?"

She lifted her chin. "Hmmm. He certainly is handsome and charming—and persuasive. Are you sure you are attracted to him or maybe gripped by the way he pays you so much attention?"

"Good question. I've certainly never had *this* kind of attention."

"Well, you wouldn't be the first woman to be in love with one man but found herself attracted to another."

I smiled at her. "My only experience is from literature and movies."

CHAPTER TWENTY-FOUR

Email to Josie

Grace to Josie:

My date with Burne is tonight. Shelta went shopping with me. I have a new dress and some, "tasteful makeup," as Shelta calls it.

I'm nervous. He's not that much older than I am, but he's so worldly. This is definitely a first date for only one of us. You asked me what work he does. I'm not sure. He seems to have a lot of money though. I got that clue from his clothes and his luxury BMW sedan. LOL

CHAPTER TWENTY-FIVE

Seductive Date

"Wow Grace, I almost didn't recognize you!"

"Thank you, Drake. I think."

We were on Seal Harbor's front deck, where I had come to walk off some of my nervousness and view the sparkling sea.

"Oh come on. There's no way you can take that as an insult. You know you look great. This," he circled his palm toward me, "did not just happen. I've never seen you wear a dress and makeup. Come to think of it, I don't think I've ever seen you out of your hoody jacket. I'm going to say it again. Wow! Where are you headed looking so fine?"

"I have a date."

His eyebrows shot up. "Who with?"

"Burne."

His eyes met mine, holding some indefinable expression, the merest shadow, no more, but I was aware of some obscure uneasiness. "I see."

"Do you? What do you see?" I smiled. "Don't you like him?"

Drake twisted his mouth before answering. "It's not that I don't like him; it's that I'm not sure I like him being with you."

The brilliance of the sun and the reflection of the water threw the large cypress tree onto the road in shadowy relief. In the distance, I saw wispy clouds moving inland.

Drake saw my eyes dart toward Burne, who had stepped up from around the corner onto the deck behind him.

"Is that right, Drake?"

The beauty of the view was eclipsed by an obvious shadow of tension. What was it that festered between these two men? Distrust? Possibly hatred? There were emotional undercurrents that seemed apparent, but I don't think I realized at first how quite strong they were. I certainly never imagined they might be dangerous.

Drake's apology revealed his gentlemanly nature. "Hi, Burne. Sorry man. Feeling a bit protective of Grace and Uny lately. It's not my place to give fatherly advice to Grace about dating."

Burne blustered a bit, I expected him to question why Drake's fatherly advice would include disapproval of him as a date for me, but to my surprise, he also chose a more gentlemanly path, "It's okay. I get it." His lips curled into an easy smile, "They do seem to need protecting, don't they?" Burne bowed his head slightly to Drake, "Will you excuse us?" He put his hand under my elbow and turned me toward the steps. "I don't need to ask you if you're ready. You look beautiful."

I did a lot of blushing around this man. "Thank you." At the bottom of the steps, I turned to Drake and sketched a wave.

As he waved bye to me, I sensed he was still not pleased.

Burne turned his attention fully toward me, "Do you need to get your bag? You'll need a sweater too. In fact, do you have a warm coat?"

"Um. Only a warm jacket. It's a sweatshirt though. Doesn't really go with my dress. Shall I ask Shelta if she has something I can borrow?"

My borrowed coat was perfect for the sunset cruise. The afternoon sunshine was bracketed by puffy clouds with cold shadows. When the crew found out that Burne was an experienced sailor, they offered him the helm. He declined their offer, waved his hand toward me, and asked them, "If you had the privilege of this beautiful woman's company, would you take your eyes off of her for any reason?" The crew nodded in varying degrees of agreement.

Of course, I blushed again.

"Is this your first time out on the ocean?"

"First time on the ocean. First time on a boat, other than a small fishing boat. First time on a date."

He jerked his head toward me and grinned. "Seriously? I am your first? I like that."

We stood on the starboard side. Watching the sea. I felt unsettled and uncomfortable. I glanced longingly at the shore behind us, wondering how long our date would be forced to last. I shivered.

"Are you cold?"

I embraced myself and rather than confess that foreboding was the true cause of my shudder, I responded, "A little."

He wore an expensive looking, black wool overcoat. From an inside pocket, he pulled a slim, silver-painted cardboard box tied with a silver satin bow. He handed it to me.

"A gift? How kind of you, but I don't know if—"

"Accept my gift. It will keep you warmer. It's my way. Don't argue. Please let me be who I am, okay?"

I pulled the end of the ribbon to untie the bow and opened the box. Within was a silk, teal and purple, artistically printed, floral scarf. "Thank you. It's beautiful."

He lifted the scarf from the box in my hands, adroitly looped it in the middle, wrapped it around my neck, and pulled the loose ends through the loop. "Yes, beautiful."

The fragrance of the sea, mingled with a misty spray, washed over us. A cluster of seagulls approached from the stern and tauntingly circled the boat. A crew member went below and returned wearing a huge grin on his face. He carried a gigantic squirt gun. A sticker on the side read, "Motion-activated water blaster." He warned us, "Whatever you do, don't be tempted to share any treats with them." He seemed to enjoy himself as he took aim and fired. One by one the gulls dropped out of the gang of wannabe moochers.

We snacked on brie, pears, grapes and stone ground wheat crackers as we tacked up the beautiful coastline of Cannery Row to Point Pinos. Burne had thoughtfully brought binoculars through which we spotted a gray humpback whale breach and blow. The captain told us it could be a mamai whale migrating with her calf, but we didn't see the baby. Burne handed me the binoculars then clasped his hands behind his back as if to keep them from mischief.

"I have to leave tomorrow." The black eyes watched me. They were unreadable as if positioned behind smoked glass.

"Oh." There I was again with one syllable and wondering why he was studying me with such intensity. "Will you be coming back to California soon?"

"Not sure." He turned his gaze over the water. "There's something unique about you, Grace. No woman has ever gotten under my skin the way you do."

This left me without even one syllable. We'd been seated and served our fresh spinach salads. I turned my full attention to balancing a walnut on my fork. It kept falling off. I finally picked it up with my fingers and popped it into my mouth.

"You've never been on a date with a man before and yet you have a captivating power over my thoughts like a vixen or a medusa."

I laughed. "A horrible, ugly monster?"

"She didn't start out that way." He smirked. The skin around his eyes creased, and his lips curved higher on one side. "Medusa was a beautiful maiden with golden hair. She vowed to be celibate her entire life as a priestess of Athena until she fell in love with Poseidon. When she broke her vow, Athena turned her into that horrible ugly monster."

A lone seagull landed on the port-side rail, stretched its wings once then settled them again upon its back. He watched us patiently, as if he'd seen us before and there was the possibility of benevolent leftovers.

The server brought our grilled Monterey Bay salmon entree.

Burne reached across the table to lift my chin so that my eyes met his. "Will you change if you fall in love?"

It was at that moment I knew I was in love with Zane. Zane accepted me for who I was, not as a goddess or a challenge or a beautiful, mythical creature with a power he needed to tame. I'd fallen in love with my friend. I said simply, "I'm positive that won't happen." I doubted that I had discouraged Burne as I wished I could.

"So sure? I've had my share of women, and they've all turned out to be monsters." His flat, dark eyes expressed disillusionment.

So smooth, so sexy, so handsome. I found it hard to believe he had merely his share of women. I supposed he'd had far more. "I'm sorry you've had such poor experiences." I truly was. "I, um, I don't know how to say this." I asked myself, *How can I be truthful yet kind?* I ached to end this date and would prefer to also end my acquaintance with Burne. Why on earth had I let this seductive man abduct me onto a boat where I was trapped until we returned to the wharf? It would be another hour before we were at dockside at Cannery Row. I said simply, "I'm not available to you."

The server brought chocolates and vanilla macarons for dessert. I spotted a dolphin off the bow to the right, but my discomfort had quashed my enthusiasm, so I neglected to point it out. The captain shooed the gull away.

Burne's eyes met mine for a moment and I felt a spark of perfect understanding.

He glowered down at the sweets. I had the sharp impression that he had not so much shut me out, but shut himself in. "I'm not used to being rejected."

Again, this was not surprising. I was grateful, however, that he understood me without my needing to fabricate some lame explanation or let-him-down-gently cliché.

If he had other thoughts, he kept them to himself. The silence that followed felt prickly. Dangerous. Dark.

The clouds went to smoky and purple at dusk before dissolving into the night sky.

CHAPTER TWENTY-SIX

Anita's Second Crisis

Anita sat on the bench, holding her phone and hugging herself, crying softly. Of course, when Cooey sent her to the psychiatrist, hoping she'd recover from depression, he had no idea what weighed so heavily on her mind. She obsessively replayed the tragedies. Daily. Hourly. Her husband didn't know that everything had been stolen from the girls on the trip she planned for them. A trip that was supposed to keep them safe and bring them happiness. She started rocking as crazy thoughts streamed through her head. Cooey only thought she was upset because the girls were gone. Anita knew him well enough to know he was angry at her for crying so often. He wanted her to stop so the life he had carefully arranged for himself would return to his control. She knew he didn't feel the devastation she felt. Angry, yes, but he was too fearful to experience other emotions that were foreign to him. The more she cried, the more he twitched and fidgeted watching her, keeping his own emotions at bay. Throughout their years together, she learned his opinion of emotions: They were a weakness. They had no place in their home or especially in business.

And now, the worst — Uny date raped and pregnant. She felt dizzy from turning her head side to side saying, "No." Then she began to moan a long, drawn out, "No," and continued to rock back and forth. Same thoughts, over and over.

"Mrs. D, are you okay?"

Anita looked up to see sweaty, breathless Zane Murphy. He had stopped running to check on her. He was leaning over with his hands on the top of his knees. Finding comfort in her rocking movement. She didn't stop. "Zane. Oh, Zane. I'm so sorry. So, so sorry."

The sun had dropped behind the buildings across the park. Zane asked her, "I can walk you home, Mrs. D. Would you like me to do that?"

Anita stared blankly toward the diminishing light and continued to rock; her tiny black cell phone was still clenched in her hand. The phone that seemed destined to bear bad news.

"Should I call someone for you?"

Fear shot through her. She enveloped the hand holding the phone with her other hand. "He can't know—he doesn't have this number."

He sat down next to her. "I'll call Mr. D from my phone, okay?" He retrieved his phone from his running shorts.

She started wailing and rocking harder and resumed shaking her head. Then she stopped wailing suddenly, and whispered, "Zane." She handed him her cell phone. "He mustn't know about this. Please keep it for me. Bring it to me when he's not around." She searched his face, thinking she understood him. "I can trust you, I know I can. You love her too, don't you?"

Zane nodded and took the tiny black phone from her hand. "Yes, Mrs. D, you can trust me, and yes. I'll call Mr. D now, shall I?" He waited for her to nod yes then placed the call. "Hi Mr. D, it's Zane Murphy. Your wife is here in the park. She needs you to come for her. Yes. She's awfully upset. She keeps rocking."

The birds in the trees above them began to sing a noisy chorus as if they were hailing the promise of coolness in the retreat of the harsh, hot sunlight.

Anita wailed above their noise, "I need to keep rocking. I need to. I rocked them. I rocked my babies. I rocked Grace. I rocked Uny. Then I rocked Johan. Oh no, oh no, oh no, my babies. I need to rock. I need to rock. I need to rock. I must rock the baby." *Oh!* She thought to herself. *Zane doesn't know about the baby. He can't find out yet. Cooey can't find out either. Zane won't tell him. Zane's a good man. What will we do about the baby? Oh, Uny. My baby is going to have a baby.*

"Yes, sir. We're at a picnic table across on the opposite side from Romp Street. Of course. I'll wait with her. I think, um, maybe bring a blanket?"

CHAPTER TWENTY-SEVEN

Zane

Zane saw Mr. Devlin running toward them on the park bench where Zane waited patiently with his hand on Mrs. Devlin's shoulder. She was still rocking and wailing about her babies. The crying had subsided to a hum.

Mr. Devlin's four-block sprint caused him to assume the same position as Zane had after his four-mile run. Mr. Devlin grasped his knees, desperately trying to fill his lungs. Running was clearly not his forté. "Hi, son. No blanket. There'll be one in the ambulance that's on the way."

Zane moved away from Mrs. Devlin, making it easy for Mr. Devlin to slide next to her and put his arms around her. A quick glance toward Zane from under puckered eyelids didn't help Zane understand Mr. Devlin's tortured expression. He wondered if Mr. D's expression was worry. Perhaps he was annoyed with her. Could that be?

"Anita, Honey. I called Dr. Clemency."

She stopped humming but continued to rock in his arms. Her voice was slurred. "Olivia?" She rocked a few times. "She asked me to call her Olivia."

"Yes. Olivia's going to meet us at the hospital."

Zane watched the ambulance pull away. He pulled Mrs. D's phone from his pocket and stared at it momentarily. He knew it contained Grace's phone number. Mrs. D didn't say he couldn't call her, but then Mrs. D was obviously not in her right mind. Maybe the phone was password protected, and he wouldn't be able to use it anyway. He slipped it into the same pocket as his phone, hoping he would have peace about whether he should use it or not after he jogged home.

He left the phone on his dresser and went to take a shower. He allowed his thoughts to wash over him as he stood beneath the warm spray that splashed on his head and ran down his lathered body. *Surely Mrs. D would want Grace to know she was in the hospital.*

The phone was not password protected. There were only two numbers in Contacts, "The Girls," and "Uny" He tapped the first number.

"Mamai! Hi! Are you okay? We just spoke—"

"This is Zane. Grace, not Uny, right?"

"Yes, it's Grace. Hi. Why are you calling from her phone? Has something happened?"

"Yes and no. She's having a breakdown of some kind. Your pa rode to the hospital with her in an ambulance a short while ago. From their conversation, I gather she's already been under a doctor's care. Her doctor was meeting them at the hospital. I found her at the table in the park. Our table, where we used to sit after a run."

"A shrink? A head doctor?"

"Yes. I think so."

"How did you get her phone?"

"She gave it to me before I called your pa from mine."

"Is she like crazy yelling or crying or something?"

"At first she was crying loudly. By the time they took her away, she was only rocking and humming. She asked me to give her back her phone when I could without your pa around." He paused intentionally. "Grace? I know this is a shock and you probably don't want me to ask you how you are or try to catch up right now, but maybe you can call me or text me when it's a good time for you?"

"Oh, Zane! Yes. Yes, of course. Please text me your number to this phone. I'm so glad you finally have my number. Our other phone was stolen." He heard a gulp followed by a deep breath. "There's so much going on. I'm wondering if Uny and I should come home. Oh gosh. That's probably not possible since nothing's changed there," she paused, "except Mamai. I don't know. This is awful. I don't know what to do. I need time to think."

"And time to pray."

"Yes, of course. And time to pray."

"I'm praying for you too. I miss you, my Miss."

"That's from your last poem." He thought he heard her voice crack with emotion as she said, "I miss you too."

"So you got them. I thought you would."

"I did." Her shaky voice dropped to a whisper. "I'll call you or at least text you back soon, Zane. I can't talk now, but thank you for letting me know about Mamai."

CHAPTER TWENTY-EIGHT

Now What?

As I tapped my phone to end the call with Zane, I felt the tears spilling hot onto my cheeks. I couldn't stop them. I had stepped out onto the oceanfront deck to take the call and balanced my caddy on the rail. I leaned over a bit, trying to compose myself. The waves blurred before me, so I focused on their hush and flow, as I strained to hear the ever-present barking of the seals. It occurred to me that if I had to feel miserable about Uny's predicament, Mamai's crisis, missing Zane, Danee, and Billy, and yes, even Pa, I was miserable in what had to be one of the most beautiful places on earth. Pacific Grove had captured my senses and my heart.

I was jerked out of my pity party trance by Drake's deep voice, "Are you okay, Grace? Sorry. I didn't mean to startle you." He lifted my caddy off the railing, pulled the tab to open a box of tissues, flipped out four of them, and handed them to me. He looked behind us into the room I'd been cleaning, put his arm around me, and directed me to sit on the stripped bed. He sat down next to me and he examined the caddy carefully as if he was not quite sure what it was. After placing it on the bed on the other side of him, he spoke gently. "It's okay. There, there, let it out."

Two shadows sailed across the way, recognizable as gulls by their whining cry. I jumped when my phone went "ding" receiving a text message. I looked at it briefly, knowing it was from Zane. No poetry, no words, only his number.

Drake's kindness accelerated, rather than stemmed, the flow of tears. I tried to take a steadying breath before speaking, but it caught somehow in my throat and sounded like a sob. I gulped it down. "Th-thank you."

He put his arm around me again and gently leaned me into his side. "You're welcome. This is what friends are for." I felt his lungs fill, as if he was showing me how. "Just breathe. It's okay, I mean, it's probably not okay, but I think it will get better." With his free arm, he grabbed the open box of tissues and placed it on my lap at the ready.

The comfortable silence and non-threatening embrace began to sooth my distress. I swallowed a couple of times and was able to breathe deeply, slowly, and say to myself, *Drake's right. I think it will get better too. It has to get better. It can't get any worse.* It helped to reassure myself, though I was entirely wrong. I sat up. "Could you please hand me the wastebasket?"

He smiled and extended his long arm to the floor next to the nightstand. "Drake the garbage man at your service."

"Drake, the man of many titles, at my service." I dropped the wad of Kleenex into the trash.

"Do you want to go rest? I can tell Shelta you're not feeling well and ask if she can send someone else to finish this room."

"No, but thank you. Getting back to work will help clear my head."

A shadow barred the sunlight streaming through the door. "So what's this?" Burne's sardonic grin indicated that either he didn't notice my blotchy face and red, swollen eyes, or he wasn't as concerned about them as he was about what could be misconstrued as intimacy. It was, of course, intimate, but not in a way that should cause Burne to be jealous.

The room was so cramped that when Drake rose from my side, he was intimidatingly near to Burne. Burne stood his ground in the shade of the taller man. The stare between them held. Big men. Serious egos. I wondered if it had always been like this between these two, or if perhaps it was about me.

Burne stepped around Drake and came to me. "I came to say good-bye." He noticed my distress. Lifting my chin, he studied my face, turning it toward the light of the window. I bit my lip and waited, not meeting his gaze. He was silent for a long time, then, as harshly as if an accusation, "You're so unhappy," then turning abruptly to Drake, "What have you done to this poor girl, Drake Bishop?"

Drake glared back, "This is not about me, Burne Crosby, nor is it about you. I'm merely Grace's friend, trying to comfort her." In the close quarters, Drake reached his hand down to me. "Come on, Grace. You need a break. I'll escort you to your room and let Shelta know this room's not done." I went through the door and turned to watch the silent warfare. Drake picked up my caddy and motioned his arm as an order to Burne to exit also. He followed Burne out, pulled the door closed, and locked it with his master key. He again put his arm around me and escorted me down the steps that led to the parking lot, leaving an enraged Burne glowering behind us.

"I'll be back in about a week. Take care of yourself, Grace."

"Bye Burne. I'll try." My other hand still clutched my phone.

CHAPTER TWENTY-NINE

Under Consideration

Uny came into the room shortly after I flopped onto my back on my bed. "Gracie! What's wrong? Drake told me I should come to see you right away."

"It's Mamai. Zane called from Mamai's phone." I told her everything Zane reported.

"What's wrong with her? Do they know? Is there a way we can we find out if we don't know?" Her voice vibrated with hysteria.

"I called her. I told her you were pregnant."

Uny fell like a heavy stone onto her bed; her breath came out in a squeak. "Oh, Grace." Her voice dropped to a low, even tone. "It's my fault. She's losing it, and it's because of me."

As I began to build her defense in my head, I realized that Uny had had a good teacher. The guilt that I carried about like a banner most of my life had taught her to respond this way. It was time to deal with my own guilt, as well as hers, in the only way it could be handled. I sat up, dangling my legs over the edge of my bed. We both needed to take responsibility for our actions, but we also needed to find freedom through the only path available. "Uny. What's happened to you may be a straw that broke the proverbial camel's back, but you cannot take the full blame for Mamai's troubled mind."

Uny continued in the depressed monotone, "I think the blame has to fall squarely on my shoulders," as if she was arguing against my logic but sought permission to believe me.

"This is not your fault, but let's say for a moment that all that has happened was entirely caused by your actions. Then what?"

She sat up on the edge of her bed, as I had on mine, and faced me. "I know what you're trying to do."

I smiled. "Do you?"

I detected a more hopeful tone in her voice, "Yes. I need to imagine the worst possible scenario and embrace it. Humbly acknowledge my responsibility. Search for peace in the most regretful, anticipated outcome. Having accepted the worst, nothing will be able to destroy that peace."

Apparently, not all my life lessons lived in front of Uny had been harmful. I smiled at her. "We have promises from God. No matter how bad a situation might seem, there are always good aspects. Remember that Bible verse in Romans, that Shelta's pastor talked about last Sunday, 'All things work together for good to those who love God, to those who are called according to His purpose?' This lesson is definitely for me also, not just you. I've pranced in front of you most of my life carrying guilt around in imaginary buckets. But God forgives me. I need to forgive myself. God is using your horrible situation and my inadequacy within it to help me grow for my good. It's a choice for both of us to lay our feelings of guilt, and all the other negative baggage that accompanies our self-centered focus, sacrificed at His feet. Not just once. We need to keep doing it, moment by moment. When we surrender our self-will, He will exchange it for the fruit of His Spirit, which includes peace and the victorious life He offers us. You know who tried to tell me that?"

"Drake?

"No, actually it was Zane."

"Just now on the phone?"

I scoffed. "No, actually he told me a long time ago when we were getting to know each other. We were talking about when his mamai died and then Collen. He said his secret to getting over guilt was to forgive himself. I should have paid closer attention. Ironically, I was too caught up in myself to listen carefully and learn from him. I'm afraid I haven't been the best example for you, especially since I've had the tools I needed all along."

She gave me an impish grin. "Actually, Grace, that's true."

I was a bit shocked to have her agree with me, but I deserved it. "You know what's scary? I'm not sure I've got this. I have a feeling I'm going to continually lapse back into self-blame."

"Well, that's a very Catholic thing to do, but we aren't Catholic anymore, right?"

"Yeah, I suppose we were brought up to think like that, but I'm not sure we're not Catholic anymore."

"Sounds like you just need to take your own advice that wasn't your advice at all. It was Zane's."

I looked at my sister with new eyes and wondered if she'd been understanding all along, or if her present suffering gave it meaning, as it had for me. "Indeed, I do need to take my own advice, and I may be the luckiest girl in the world to have you as my sister."

Her eyes gleamed with wetness. "Or maybe I'm the lucky one to have a sister to remind me that the fight for faith is never over. It's an ongoing, moment by moment, victory built on surrender."

I moved to her side of the room and hugged her. "We'll get through this. We may need to go to her, but Mamai will get through this too, somehow."

CHAPTER THIRTY

Emails with Josie

Grace to Josie:

I feel defeated. I may have to take Uny home. My mamai is losing her mind over Uny and I know Uny wants to go to her. You'd never guess how I found out about Mamai: Zane called me from Mamai's phone! He found her in a hot mess on a park picnic bench on the way back from his run. She had just hung up from her call with me. I told her about Uny being pregnant. Zane called Pa. Pa called an ambulance. She's in the hospital.

I am excited to hear from Zane. I actually do think what we have between us might be love. I realized it, at the craziest time: when I was out with Burne.

Burne took me on an ocean cruise. At first I was thrilled to be out on the ocean for the first time. But, as the evening progressed, I felt trapped, wishing I could return to shore and say goodnight. I'm not sure how to summarize this, but I'll give it a shot. I felt like our conversation was a verbal tennis match, him trying to score points, and me deflecting them. He confessed that other women he had known had turned into monsters. He was afraid I would also. It was confusing. There were compliments in abundance, but it also seemed as if he wanted to manipulate me and change me. I found myself longing for the partnership of running in rhythm with Zane, hearts, breath, and steps in sync.

Josie to Grace:

I keep wondering, how can so many things be happening to you? I guess the good news is, it can't get any worse!

First of all, from this distance, I don't think you need to feel defeated. Just because these things have happened, it doesn't mean you were wrong to take a stand by leaving. Who on earth could stand to marry the father of the man they love and live in the same house?

Wow on the date with Burne and the epiphany about Zane. I mean, just wow!

You know my situation. I'm learning that what happened to me is not nearly as important as how I respond to it. Thanks to you, my dad, and Kris, I believe I have a future that doesn't need to be defined by my past.

This can be true for you too. Especially for Uny and possibly for your mom also. I don't have all the answers, but I'm thinking you could go home now, not in defeat but with hope that God will guide you to something better.

CHAPTER THIRTY-ONE

Connected to Zane and Home

"I knew something was wrong when a guy with a gravelly voice answered your phone."

Hearing Zane say this brought back the memory of Smelly Dude. "Yeah. I think I know who that was. A guy and his wife or girlfriend, both heavy smokers, sat in front of us on the Los Angeles leg of the trip. Uny and I fell asleep. When we woke up in LA, our phone and everything else were stolen. The baggage redemption ticket that I'd stashed in the front pocket of my backpack made it easy for them to steal our luggage also."

Zane confessed, "I have to admit I was relieved when he hung up on me without asking for ransom."

"Oh gosh, Zane. I never thought of that!"

"That's when I wrote the first poem that I sent to *The Pine*. The one about loss."

"How did you know where to send it?"

"It's the only local paper in the Monterey and Carmel area."

I laid there in the warm afternoon silence on my bed where I had settled before I texted Zane and asked if this was a good time for a phone chat. He called me back immediately. I'd left the door open. I loved that the windows didn't need screens, that I could leave doors open, and I hadn't seen a filthy fly since I'd arrived in Pacific Grove. My not-so-exceptional-view out the door was the Inn parking lot that ended at a fence, perpendicular to the driveway to Ocean View Boulevard. The light streamed into the room, reminding me that though the Inn seemed to be facing west, Pacific Grove was actually on the southern curve of the Monterey Bay, so it faced north. The westerly afternoon sun streamed sunshine onto the foot of my bed. A bird, small and bright as a blown leaf, flew across the hot stillness of the asphalt then swooped toward the coolness on the opposite side of the ocean-front wing.

Uny was working. I didn't know how long she would hold up. She could show up at any time needing to rest or possibly to barf. Her pregnancy was beginning to be a bit bumpy.

"It took me a few weeks to notice your poems, but I looked up the other two." It felt awkward mentioning his love poems, so I volleyed a topic shift. "Have you heard how my mamai is?"

"No, Sorry. I went to the hospital hoping to sneak her phone back to her, but the hospital staff prevented me. She wasn't receiving visitors. I called your pa, but he didn't answer the phone. I asked my pa to keep trying to reach him."

"My pa may have seen your name in his phone and didn't answer because he is embarrassed."

"I thought of that. I left him a voice mail."

"Zane, do you think he *should* be embarrassed?"

"No, um, yeah. I mean, I don't think it's right. Unfortunately, I know the mindset of the Traveler men. Your mamai was emotional in public. He probably sees that as a poor reflection on him."

"Exactly. He definitely sees emotion, particularly a public display of emotion, as a failure, but *her* failure. I'm equally sure he thinks everything that has happened, our running away and mamai's breakdown, is all about him. That's the way he's been my whole life. Any of our accomplishments, few as they have been, are his. Any of our failures are not his fault but are definitely an embarrassment to him."

"Not just him, you know."

I heard a bitter tone in my reply. "I know. What about you, Zane? If you get married, will you consider your family an extension of your ego?" As soon as I asked, I regretted my words. "Wait! Don't answer that. That was mean and spectacularly unfair. You've already opened up enough for me to know you're breaking the mold the Traveler men set for you."

"Thank you, Grace. I am different than most of the Traveler men and I'm not all that different than you, you know?"

"Me? Gypsy Grace?"

He chuckled. "I like it. Gypsy Grace wandering to the Pacific Ocean to become a famous writer."

"Famous writer or chambermaid?"

"It'll happen. You're an artist. We're both artists in our own way. It makes us different than others. We're driven by some compulsion that tells us if we can't do what we know we have to do with our lives, we may as well be dead."

I scoffed. "I'm not sure I'm as committed to my writing as unto death. Are you really that driven by your music and poems?"

"Well, I guess not to death, but I definitely have the stereotypical moody artist's personality. And the drama. I suppose that's why I chose the word 'death.' My emotions move in waves that stir me. Even when I'm working, or especially when my mind is droning on during a mundane task, a poetic or musical inspiration often awakens and prods me. I grab my phone and text a message to myself at my email address. I have to be more adroit when creativity strikes in the shower."

I laughed. "Sounds like you need a waterproof phone."

"I've been more inclined to wander in my creativity since you've been gone."

Here again was the mention of his love poems. I didn't have the heart to do another topic shift, but neither did I feel adequate to respond.

"Does your silence mean I'm alone? At one point, I was confident this is a two-sided friendship; am I wrong?"

"Actually, I've had an epiphany." As soon as the words were out of my mouth, I realized that explaining the why and where could be awkward.

"Epiphany, I like the sound of that, I think."

"The conclusion you will like, although you may not enjoy all the details surrounding its advent."

Now it was I who listened to silence, as if he was deciding what he was willing to hear. As I waited for his reply, three birds hung above the butterfly bush on the other side of the fence. They circled slowly with motionless wings, like some mobile toy on an invisible thread. A butterfly, apparently unafraid of the small birds, hovered over the bush then landed and clung to one of the purple, brush-shaped cones poking into a strip of sunlight. The butterfly wings, black velvet shot with gold, folded gently together.

His deep breath sounded much like a sigh. "I think I'll take the summary sans painful details."

"Okay. That's fair. I'll try. If your feelings for me are strong though, I'll—"

"They are."

I continued. "The story may still inflict some pain. You see, someone here has found me attractive."

"I find that's easy to believe. Did you? Um, no. I won't ask. Go on."

"Well, the thing is, I realized while he was making his moves on me that he was also prepping me to change. While he was trying to manipulate me into being what he wanted me to be and essentially change me into what he wanted or needed. He also kept complimenting me for who I am warning me not to change. I felt confused."

"Sounds confusing."

"During his muddled attempt to woo me, I recognized the genuine quality of the connection I have with you."

Zane agreed. "Epiphany indeed."

Chapter Thirty-two

Discovery

"Grace. I'm going out this afternoon, and Hogan has a late exercise class with his ladies. It would be a good time for you to clean the upper office. The key to the office is on the pegboard next to the kitchen door. It's labeled, 'UPPER.'"

Halfway up the stairs, I realized I was too early; Crosby was still there. I heard his voice and I took a few steps down but stopped dead on a stair when I heard him say Pa's name. I tiptoed back up, closer to the door. "This will be harder than Collen's. He doesn't work the roads, but it also needs to look like an accident. There are also the others. Devlin and Murphy play golf together. Maybe we could arrange something for two of them or even all three." I felt my heart pounding in my ears. I took a deep breath and carefully placed my right foot on the stair beneath me. Before I shifted my weight, I heard him say, "Yeah, to start with. Maybe that'll work. Think about it. So will I. I gotta go. I've got a class." I sprinted down the stairs, jumping over the one at the bottom, which had creaked on my way up. I rounded the corner at the bottom and darted quickly into my room, feeling grateful I'd left the door unlocked. I held it open a crack and listened for the thrust of the bolt in the upper office door, his descent of the stairs, and his footfalls reaching the carport.

I was a hot mess. I gently closed the door, turned around, and leaned back. I took deep breaths, trying to compose myself. There was a siren in my head. With every heartbeat, my palms and fingers pulsed against the door's veneer. I was trying to think my way out of what I'd heard. *Who could he be talking to? Apparently, Crosby's life insurance policy on Collen wasn't only because he was his godfather. I had forgotten Aislyn was Paddy's sister. That means he probably has a policy on Paddy and Zane who would be "the others". For sure he has a target on Pa's back. He must have an insurable interest in Pa because of Mamai's family connection with Shelta.* I threw my body onto my bed and held my screaming head. *I have to warn Pa, but I can't talk to him. At least I can warn Zane. Oh no, oh no, oh no. Maybe I didn't hear Crosby right.* I replayed each word on the recorder in my brain. If I were going to go to the police, I would need some kind of proof so it wouldn't be just my word against his.

We all have those moments that are meant to test us and change us; to make plain what it means to risk everything. I needed to be brave.

I got up from my bed, ran my hands through my hair, took the "UPPER" key from my pocket, and headed back up the stairs to the private office.

The well-organized hand of Shelta was evident on the desk and in the carefully labeled inserts of the file cabinets. I sat down at the desk and took in the essence of the room. I was sweating. I stood up, took off my jacket and draped it around the back of the desk chair and then sat back down. The contents of the center drawer was uncluttered and functional. Letter opener, paper clips in a magnetic box, scissors, pens, an old-fashioned calculator with large buttons. Two top drawers on the left were equally orderly, but the deeper, file-sized drawer beneath it was a mess. On top of the stack of papers was a laminated badge of some sort with Crosby's picture. It was attached to a blue lanyard. This had to be Crosby's drawer. If there was evidence that what happened to Collen was not an accident, it could be here. I cleared the center of the desktop by sliding the few functional items on the top of the desk off to the right, set the lanyard badge alongside them, and lifted out a deep stack of documents. There was room to turn the pages upside down, creating a new stack after skim reading each piece. The dates seemed to indicate each paper had been chronologically dropped on top. I counted back. Uny and I arrived at Seal Harbor about four months ago. That would put Collen's accident about six months before that. *October? Really? So hot, but yes, the Texan meteorologists called it an Indian summer.* Digging by handfuls, checking the dates. I carefully turned each stack over so I could put them back exactly the way they were. Before I reached the October papers, I found it. My eyes traced over the document a second time, and then a third. It was a bill from Rent-a-Wreck for a white, Ford pickup truck originally rented October 12, but never returned. Attached was a November receipt paid by HB Enterprises. Crosby reimbursed the company for the truck's entire replacement price.

My hand went for the phone in the pocket of my jacket on the chair behind me. I tapped the camera, but remembered Zane's phone wasn't a smartphone. The paper shook in my hand as stood up to face the copier on the credenza across from the desk. It was not just a copier. It was also a fax machine. I slid the receipt into the top feeder and called Zane.

I glanced at the time. *He's two hours ahead.* "Are you still at work?"

"Hi, Grace. Yes, workin' a little late. Are you okay? You sound shaky. What's up?"

"Sorry. Little time to explain. I've got to hurry. Do you have a fax machine?"

"Yes."

"Do you know the number?"

"No, but I'll get it. Just a sec. I need to roll out from under this Benz and walk over to the office. It's printed on our business cards."

"Can you please text it to me?" I'm going to fax something to you. I'll call later, as soon as I can. I need to put stuff away and get out of here."

"Stuff? Out of where? Um. Okay."

"Zane?"

"It's something frightening. Remember the white truck that killed Collen?"

"Yes. I remember. They never found it."

"Right, but I found a receipt for the rental of one that matches the description. What's worse is, the reason I searched for it and found it is because I overheard Crosby on the phone talking to someone about my pa dying in an accident that would need to be different than Collen's. My pa is in immediate danger and possibly you and your pa too. I may ask you to warn my pa. I don't know what to do. I have to figure this out. If you tell him, he'll know you know where I am and that you're in touch with me. Oh dear, it's so complicated! I'm not sure what we *can* do, but what I know for sure is right now is; I really need to hurry."

My phone dinged. "Oh good! Got the number. Thank you." Without giving him a chance to respond, I tapped the red hang-up phone symbol and typed the number from Zane's text into the fax keyboard. The receipt sucked painfully, slowly into the feeder. At first, I thought nothing was happening until I heard a dial tone. The machine blurted out a series of beeps and boops then started to screech.

I retrieved the paper at the end of its journey and sat back down at the desk, dropping my phone into my jacket pocket. A shadow crossed over my hand that held the bill and receipt. I looked up and saw Crosby blocking the sunlight from the doorway, sending the blood out of my heart with a contraction as painful as a blow.

CHAPTER THIRTY-THREE

Busted and Bound

"Wha? Grace! What are you doing here?" Crosby crossed the room in three long strides and clamped my wrist with his left hand. He jerked the paper out of my hand and intensified his grip when he recognized what it was. "No!"

"Ow, Crosby, you're hurting me!"

The chair swiveled and stopped with a thud when the arm of the chair collided with the desk. He turned reached across the aisle and dropped the papers onto the copier paper tray. With his free hand, he wrenched open a drawer beneath the copier and grabbed a dispenser of clear packing tape. Twisting my arm behind my back, he forced me to sit sideways. He mumbled something like, "Lucky thing I forgot my lanyard."

What happened next, would have made me laugh if I hadn't been terrified. Anyone who as ever tried to use packing tape one-handedly, or even with both hands when in a hurry, would appreciate Crosby's frustration. The simple dispenser was merely a four inch roll of tape with teeth sticking out of one side. Teeth more likely to scratch or puncture the user than efficiently cut tape. Still holding me painfully immobile, he used one finger on the hand that was gripping me to steady the tape dispenser and his other hand to yank a strip of the tape out in front of me. It awkwardly tangled into an unusable tube. He cursed and ripped the end across the dispenser's jagged teeth. A portion of the unwieldy cylinder floated in the air and stuck to my shoulder. The other end attached itself to Crosby's hairy arm. He tried again; this time he was a little more successful but not much. I saw his hand come around to my face where he slapped a small, usable section over my mouth. A snake of tape trailed on each side of my face.

How stupid I had been not to scream.

He brought my twisted arm to the front and grabbed both of my wrists together in his huge hand. He used the curled tubes of tape as a rather clumsy rope, first wrapping, and then tying my wrists together. A sickening stench lingered in his workout clothes and magnified with his exertion. He pushed my body into place in the chair and held me there with his forearm. He grunted and yanked long strips of tape which he used to attach me firmly to the chair. With both hands free, he was more successful with the tape and dispenser. I think he realized my jacket might slide and give me some freedom of movement. He connected a strip of tape to a rung beneath the chair, wrapped it across my lap, and affixed it to another rung on the other side. The tape shrieked with each violent lug, rip, and slice of the teeth.

I'm convinced that he not only read my thought, but he was thinking the same thing. *Now what?*

His face was sweaty and beet red. His hands were shaking as he picked up the bill and receipt again. He paced in the small space between the front and back walls of the office, mumbling to himself or perhaps thinking he was telling me how futile my efforts were. "No paper in the copier. I knew that. So she's the only one who's seen this." He stared at the papers a few seconds and paced a few more times before looking over my left shoulder.

I shot him a look that I hoped conveyed how stupid I thought he was. He hadn't heard the fax. Hopefully, he wouldn't notice the last number dialed. As if the fax machine wanted him to notice, it beeped as a tiny light blinked off.

He spun to look at the machine, but apparently didn't think it was unusual for it to beep after making a copy. He drew his phone from his pocket, tapped a button, and breathed heavily as he waited for a response. "Yeah. Where are you? Are you close? We have a problem. No, not that problem. We'll have to wait on that. Can't have that many accidents so close together. This problem is here. Don't park at the Inn. Find somewhere nearby. Public. Not a suspicious side street either. Your car is too noticeable. Yeah, good idea. They'll assume you're at the restaurant." He paused listening. "How long do you think? Maybe you should stop to get a quick sandwich or something. It's going to be a long night. When you get to town, come straight to my upstairs office. If possible, try to avoid being seen by people we know. I'm going down to dinner with the family so they won't wonder where I am. I'll come up here as soon as we're done. It soon will be dark."

CHAPTER THIRTY-FOUR

A Bit of Mercy

My wrists, my mouth, and my arms passed the place where pain converted into tingling numbness. My bottom ached where I was forced to sit without the ability to adjust the poor posture into which I'd been taped. I sensed my phone in the pocket of my jacket. So near, yet so far away. I knew it was still on Do Not Disturb because I always use DND when I'm driving. I had recently returned from town. Uny could be texting or calling, but my phone would politely stay silent as I had asked it to. I wondered if Crosby had manufactured some possibility of why I was not at dinner for the sake of Shelta, Uny, and Ryker, or if he was looking over their shoulders, playing the clueless card. Probably the latter.

When the door finally opened, it was not Crosby. It was Burne. He looked shocked.

He came to me quickly and struggled with the tape on the chair. I looked at him and darted my eyes to the desk drawer. He took my cue and found the scissors. He cut the tape beneath the chair first and then proceeded to where Crosby had taped over the tangled, snake-like jumble on my wrists. He wrenched it away with a familiar, stick-to-his-hands struggle, as his father before him. Persistently, he snipped, pulled and snipped again, being careful not to poke or slice my skin. When he left my mouth covered, I realized he was the person Crosby had called; the one who Crosby was talking to about Collen's "accident;" Crosby's partner plotting my pa's death. HB Enterprises. *Hogan Burne?* Unless there were others involved, he would have been the one who drove the white truck from California to Texas to murder Collen, while his father stayed in Pacific Grove with an alibi seventeen hundred miles away.

I rubbed my wrists as I simultaneously stood. I heard a soft, remorseful groan as Burne rubbed the sides of my arms and took me into his arms for a gentle hug. He smelled clean and wore a discriminating dose of aftershave. I thought I heard him whisper above my head, "No."

Crosby came through the door and shut it quickly behind him. He looked over our hugging bodies in the general direction of Burne's left shoulder. "What are you doing?"

"Hugging Grace," he said simply, but then he released me. I began again to rub my wrists. I wished I could also rub my back and my bottom, but I guess I was more ladylike than I had always considered myself to be.

"You need to get her out of here."

"Pa, what is this? What's going on?"

Burne recognized the receipt Crosby had placed into his hand. The dark eyes, under the perfect arch of his prominent brows, seemed solid, opaque black, without pupils, without light from within. His chin jerked toward me. He shook his head, groaning and whispering softly again, "No."

It occurred to me that as Crosby's partner in murder, it was no wonder he seemed so lonely. Murderers must be the loneliest people in the world. It's the curse of Cain, the fugitive and vagabond, driven out from the face of the earth. I remembered reading a Proverb in my new Bible, "A man tormented by the guilt of murder will be a fugitive till death." However Burne might try to justify it, he had parted company with the rest of humanity the moment the truck he was driving hit Collen on that Texas highway. His groans were probably because he didn't want to kill me. However, because he had killed one person, he had passed beyond where most people would ever tread. To kill two or more would make no difference. The man who stood next to me now was no longer the man who overwhelmed me with romantic attention. Crosby's side of the phone conversation I had overheard, and the evidence I found, would force Burne to disregard all natural emotion. He would have to kill me to silence me.

My heart was beating so loudly I could hear it. My head was buzzing like a radio that had lost track of its signal.

Then Burne surprised me with more kindness. He touched the outside of my reddened arm. "Are you hungry? Do you need to use the bathroom?"

I nodded my head.

"Okay. Come with me."

Crosby growled, "Burne! What are you doing? You know what has to be done!"

Burne replied, "Sadly, Pa, I do, but I care about Grace, and I'm going to take her to my room so she can freshen up. Then I'm going to feed her before I take her for a ride."

Crosby looked directly into Burne's dark eyes and poked him in the chest. Apparently he was able to look someone directly in the eyes when he was furious. "Don't blow this, Burne. Don't you dare exchange her life for ours."

Burne grabbed the finger that was poking him and repositioned his father's hand to his side.

Burne lifted my jacket from the chair, draped it around my shoulders, put his arm around me, and escorted me to the door. He peered out. He held me firmly at his side as he led me down the stairs and into the parking lot. It wouldn't be dark for a while, but a thin mist was rolling in from across the bay. There would be a glorious sunset. Unfortunately, there was no one to see him escort me to the room that was customarily his, located at the far inland end of the Inn's non-ocean-front wing.

"If I removed this, will you promise not to scream?"

As I nodded my head, I wondered how bound I would be to keep my word to someone who intended to murder me.

"Sorry, I'm going to rip it off quickly." And he did. He set the end of the tape onto the top of the dresser with the remainder sticking out as if ready for reuse.

He removed my jacket from my shoulders, gently laid it onto his bed, and tilted his head toward the bathroom. It took incredible effort not to glance at the bed; for me to ignore the presence of my phone lying there out of my control.

I splashed water on my hands and face. It hurt to bend the bruised wrist that Crosby manhandled hours before. The water stung the flesh yanked raw from the tape, but I welcomed its promise of healing relief. As far as I could reach around myself, I massaged my bottom and the aching muscles on my sides, shoulders, and back. A sharp remedial tingling seemed to signal my body's return from whatever numb borderlands of shock in which I had been residing. How was I going to play this? Would I go quietly like a lamb to the slaughter? Should I thrash him with my anger and indignation? The only thing I knew for sure was that I needed to pray.

CHAPTER THIRTY-FIVE

Abduction

I stopped to listen before opening the bathroom door. Burne was speaking softly, but I have good ears. "There aren't any high cliffs around here. Yeah, but if they find her body near Carmel and they figure out who she is, how will they explain how she got that far away? Right. Okay, I suppose that's true. I gotta go. It's quiet. I think she's coming out."

I took a deep breath, set my back and shoulders straight, lifted my chin, and stepped out of the bathroom to face my murderer. The room smelled like heavenly pizza. I spotted the box sitting on the side table between two upholstered chairs. I was hungry. "Thank you for your kindness."

His agate eyes stared back at me from an expression that was difficult to read. It was stern but not angry. Determined, I supposed. He was resolved to murder me, but somehow equally determined to continue to be kind to me. He motioned to the chair farthest from the door, picked up the few paper plates on top of the box, handed me a double layer, and offered the open box. "Please eat. You must be starving. This is all I could think of that could get here quickly."

The ambiguity of his last word hung between us. Quickly, because he knew I was hungry. Quickly, so he could get this over with. Take me for a ride.

He walked over to a small ice chest adjacent to the night table and retrieved a chilled bottle of water. He set the water and a few napkins next to me on the table then reached into the box for a slice of pizza for himself. He sat down in the chair between me and the exit.

We ate in silence.

I glanced toward him frequently, purposely maintaining perfect posture and manners. I kept my knees together like a refined lady. I intended to challenge him by looking directly into his eyes, but he didn't look up. His posture and demeanor were not as confident as the shell I was projecting. With each bite, he studied his slice of pizza. When he finished eating, he looked up. "Are you done?"

Again ambiguity hissed through the room.

I rose. "May I wash up before we go?"

"Yes."

He was waiting outside the bathroom door. He draped my jacket around my shoulders and firmly bound his left arm around my shoulders. He pulled the tape from the dresser and returned it to my stinging face, covering my mouth. Before I realized what he was doing, he had both of my wrists in one hand and was taping them together with a piece of tape he'd had at the ready on the dresser. He whispered, "I'm sorry."

Clutching me intensely to his side, he ushered me to the door. Something rigid bit into my side. In spite of my throbbing fear and physical discomfort, I again noticed his aftershave. He opened the door, looked around, and escorted me around the back of the building and then marched us across the street. He shifted me to the inside of the sidewalk. He held me so tightly, I could barely breathe.

Typical Pacific Grove, evening quietness had settled. If someone saw us huddled closely together, it would appear that we both wanted to be. Just another romantic couple snuggling on a cool shoreline walk. No one close enough to see the clear tape across my mouth or binding my wrists.

We continued our synchronized steps to the corner and then turned right, away from the Inn onto Ocean View Boulevard. I caught a glimpse of Drake on the front deck of Seal Harbor's front office and mentally commended Burne for retaping my mouth. Burne apparently saw him also. It seemed unbelievable to me that he could squeeze me firmer, but he did, and he picked up our pace. We turned abruptly into a courtyard-like parking area at an ocean-front motel with restaurant parking. A late-flying seagull screeched above us as Burne forced me onto the passenger seat of his BMW. He jerked the roll of packing tape from his inside pocket. This then, was what had jabbed me. With far more finesse than his father, he wrapped tape behind the bucket seat and snugly around my torso. He closed the passenger door. Taped to the luxury leather, I waited in the stillness. He opened the driver's side door and slid behind the wheel. He looked spent. His handsome face was flushed and clammy. The heat from his body caused his once alluring aftershave to fill the car's cabin. He steadied his shaky hands, placing them on the steering wheel, and bowed his head. After taking a deep breath, he lifted his head and started the car. As we were rolling backward toward the exit, he braked. He looked at me with what I can best describe as doleful, puppy dog eyes and reached across to rip the tape from my mouth.

"Ow." This rip was considerably more painful than the previous one. The skin around my mouth pulsated in response to the air that felt like fire, I flinched my head down and futilely attempted to bend my bound arms up toward my face to rub the abused, sensitive skin.

"I know. I'm sorry." He turned north out of the courtyard, but unexpectedly turned right at the corner and right again, so that we were heading south toward Carmel, adroitly driving in that direction without passing Seal Harbor Inn.

The foaming waves continued their relentless journey to the shore. The birds sat on their rocks or circled. Life would go on the same for them after I was executed.

I felt anger curling in my belly. "It was you who killed my fiancé."

Burne twitched his head toward me. I sensed rather than saw that I had hit a nerve. Perhaps he still had a remnant of conscience. He turned his attention back to the road and asked, "You were engaged to Paddy's son?"

My throat was suddenly dry. I heard myself say in a strange voice, "Yes. I don't suppose a murderer stops to think about how taking the life of one person affects the lives of so many others."

The BMW's smooth engine, the gentle flow of the wind through the partially open windows, the distant shrill of sea birds, and the ocean's throb emphasized his silence. I thought he was done talking. When he finally answered. His voice was monotone and emotionless, the way Mamai's voice sounded when she was in the depths of depression. "I followed a plan. Followed orders. Not my plan. I got paid. Truthfully, I tried not to think about it too much."

"Were you partially responsible for your mother's accidental death on motel stairs also?"

His head jolted toward me once more. The black brows snapped together and the hard, dark eyes looked straight through my brain to scrape the back of my skull, then he returned his attention to the upward winding road. His voice was loud and tight, "That *was* an accident!"

"Was it?"

Silence again. The knuckles on his hands turned white as he clenched the blood from them in his grip on the steering wheel. Muscles in his face and throat went taut. "I wasn't there. I loved my mamai." He blinked his eyes a couple of times but continued to stare at the road, which had veered closer to the shore where the waves were higher than I had seen them in all the months I had lived close to the beach. Their forever journey to crash and spray upon the shoreline rocks caused me to sink deeply into meditations of my eternal Father of creation. I found courage.

He uttered quietly, almost more as a statement than a question, "You think my pa killed the mother of his children?"

"I know your pa murders for money, and I know he got a lot of it when your mother died."

The veins at the top of his hands popped up vividly as he gripped the steering wheel more intensely. He was silent, but it was a thick silence as if the car filled with an emotional angry mist. A forest engulfed the road, stealing the view of the sun making its descent into the bay. I took a last longing look through the remaining gaps in the tree trunks, the red of the sky that was deepening to copper and the glimmer of water that recalled the copper sky. It caused sadness as only goodbyes can. I had seen Uny, Shelta, and Ryker for the last time. *I will never see Mamai, Pa, Danee, Billy, or Zane again.* Emotion swelled into my throat and eyes. *Will someone else pray for them every day after I'm gone? Who will pray for Josie? Mamai will go into her mind and never return. I wanted to be there for Uny when she delivered her baby. This is my last sunset.* I felt hot tears sting the raw skin on my cheeks. My bound hands, with no access to a tissue, left me with no choice but to stay true to my unladylike ways. I sniffed a few times to restrain the dripping waterworks.

The car veered to a sharp right and began to climb a narrow, poorly maintained road. The potholes got deeper and closer together as the road became steeper and leveled out to a small rocky plateau. Burne stopped the car and pressed a button to lower the windows entirely. The cool salty air cleansed the car's cabin. The Pacific was in front of the windshield. The setting sun rimmed the clouds in blazing gold and the sea was moaning below the cliffs. A rocky cliff was to our left. Seeming to defy nature, a lone cypress stood atop the rock.

In a depressed, monotone voice he declared. "We're here."

"This is where there's going to be an accident?"

He turned in his seat to face me and started futilely worrying at the tape that bound me to the bucket seat. Muttering an expletive, he reversed position in his bucket seat, pulled a lever beneath the steering wheel, opened his driver's door and got out. I heard him rummaging in the trunk. I watched the gold fade from the clouds. They changed shapes and shades as they drifted into darkness. My door opened. Burne tackled the tape with a screwdriver until it broke, then he ripped it from my body. He slipped his arm behind my shoulders and gently lifted me to my feet. He used the screwdriver in a similar way to free my hands. For a moment, we stood facing each other; me rubbing my wrists; him staring over my shoulder at the ocean. We were standing close enough together that he could have easily grabbed me if

I tried to run. While I was calculating my chances, with another of those improbable looks that seemed to go past the eyes straight into my mind, he declared. "It's not going to be your accident."

"What do you mean?"

"The keys are in the car. Go home, get your sister, and flee before my father sees you."

"You want me to leave you here?"

"I'm going to do a Jack Sparrow swan dive off that cliff." He pointed to the top of the hill. "Except unlike his dive, there's no water beneath that one, only rocks."

"No, Burne. No." I shook my head and leaned through a cloud of aftershave to grab his hands. I pressed them tightly together between my own. "Thank you for sparing me, but don't do this. Please don't do this. It wasn't your greed."

"Yes, it partially *is* my greed, but I don't deserve a pardon for my actions. I essentially ended my life when I killed your fiancé. What am I going to do with the rest of my life? If I don't dive off that cliff, they'll kill me anyway, or I'll be locked in a prison cell. I deserve it. You know, a life for a life."

An entire flock of birds filled the cypress tree whose roots seem to thrive in solid rock. They chirped loudly in the semi-darkness.

"You believe in God, and you believe in the Bible?"

He looked at me. "I do. My mother taught me, even though the Church wasn't all that approving of us reading it and learning it. You wouldn't think I do, after what I've done, would you? But I do. I suppose for a time I changed my beliefs to justify my behavior. Now I realize I need to adjust my behavior to honor my beliefs. Thank you." He scoffed. "It's you, Grace. You did this. You reminded me of who I was, who my mamai wanted me to be."

"And you think diving to your death off a cliff will honor your beliefs and your mamai?"

He broke away from the grip I had on his hands, straightened his shoulders, and smoothed back his hair. He took a few steps toward the cliff.

I pleaded with more confidence and authority than I felt, "Wait! Burne! Your pa will get away with it. You need to come back to testify against him so he can't kill anyone else."

He stopped still. Still facing away from me he muttered, "Like your pa?"

"Yes. Like my pa. I think he was supposed to be next until I got moved up in the queue."

"You can tell them I told you."

"No."

He turned and smiled for the first time since he'd walked into the upper office several hours before. "No?"

"Right. No. This is your victory and your purpose. You believe in God and His Son, Jesus, right?"

"Yes."

"Then you know He forgives those who are contrite, and He uses broken people. He even uses people in prison. You need to get to know Him. To know Him is to know His love. With His love, we no longer have shame and separation no matter what we've done, no matter what we regret. On our way here, I was thinking if you killed me," I saw Burne wince and hang his head, "I wondered who would take my place praying for the people I pray for every day. What if you stood in the gap between Earth and Heaven to pray for people every day? There are so many who need someone faithfully praying for them. Ryker and your other siblings. Shelta. And your Pa."

He slowly lifted his eyes to mine, seeking something in my gaze. Redemption, forgiveness, or permission. "What is it about you? How do you do that? You turn the worst possible scenario into something positive." He came back to where I was standing, lifted my chin, kissed my cheek, and smoothed it with his fingers before he picked me up and hugged me.

Headlights from an approaching car shined as a spotlight on my dangling feet. Uniformed officers stepped out with their weapons drawn. Burne set me down and turned toward the guns with his hands up in surrender.

I lifted my hands as well. "Don't shoot. Please don't shoot him. He was just hugging me. He wasn't trying to hurt me."

The birds in the cypress tree ceased their incessant chirping. The world turned silent except for the moan of the waves below and a tiny scuffling of a dry twig that the breeze was patting idly along the rocks. One of the policemen lowered his gun and opened the back door of the squad car. Drake unfolded his long body onto the path.

Drake drove me back to the Inn in Burne's BMW.

"You saw us, didn't you? When Burne was marching me to his car?"

"Yes. I thought it was you, and he was abducting you. Uny called me when you didn't show up for dinner. I knew for certain it was you after I ran behind you and plastered myself against the wall in front of the restaurant. I got his license plate number when he turned north. He didn't see me. I called the police and asked them to meet me at the Inn. Intuitively, I felt I should not send the police to Crosby at the Inn. I asked them to meet me on the corner. I went to your room where Uny said she'd be, and asked if I could see her phone. I remembered that you set up a way to track each other's phones in case one got misplaced."

"My phone and I certainly were misplaced! So you followed us in the police car using my GPS?" A huge realization almost took my breath away. "Crosby must have been in such shock to find out I was onto him that it didn't occur to him that I had my phone in my jacket pocket." I stared down at the screen in my palm. "I have a lot of missed calls and texts from Uny; some of them would be when I missed dinner, the rest when I was with Burne in his room and in the car on the way to the cliff. Burne and I didn't hear anything because I had it on DND." I looked at him and smiled. "And, God was gracious. The battery indicator is red. Down to ten percent. It would have been impossible to follow me much longer."

"They don't seem to be very experienced criminals."

"Oh, I think they've got more experience than anyone should ever have, especially Crosby."

"I heard you telling the police you overheard him talking about how your fiancé's death was not an accident and you found proof."

"Yes. I faxed the evidence to Zane and told him I had overheard Crosby say that my Pa needed to have a different accident than Collen had. Even if they had successfully murdered me, I think a jury would consider a receipt for a missing truck matching the one that killed Collen, and a huge insurance policy payout, and my hearsay conversation with Zane compelling. But Burne is going to testify against his pa now too."

We had reached Forest Avenue that fell away to Ocean View Boulevard. Drake parked two blocks from Seal Harbor to give the police time to arrest Crosby. In spite of the mist, the shoreline was visible. The light from the buildings across Ocean View Boulevard streamed out into the steamy vaporous air and threw a murky shifting radiance across the street and onto the pulsing waves.

"I don't think Burne had anything to do with his mother's accident, but I suspect Crosby may have. I don't know. It may have really been an accident, but when Crosby got both an insurance payoff plus recompense from the motel where she fell, it may have fueled his greed."

"Holy cow! If your suspicions are correct, Shelta may have been in danger too."

"I know, right? I warned her that I thought it was a possibility."

"So you were engaged to someone named Collen?"

"I'd call it betrothed, not engaged. We hardly knew each other. Our fathers arranged it."

"That seems so weird in this day and age."

"Yes, and it gets weirder. Zane is Collen's brother."

"Oh, I see." He tilted his head. "Did you and Zane start liking each other before—"

"Wait! It's weirder than that. No. I only started getting to know Zane at Collen's funeral. After Zane and I started seeing each other, my pa betrothed me to Zane's pa."

"No way!"

"Way and ew! I would have lived under the same roof with both of them. It's a gypsy thing." I giggled for the first time all day. It was probably hysteria. "That's why Uny and I are here. Our mamai helped us escape to her Cousin Shelta."

"There's an ancient cliché for this, you know, 'Out of the frying pan and into the fire.' Oh look, the police are coming out with Crosby. Let's go." He started the purring engine of Burne's BMW. "Uny needs to see you. Shelta may need you more."

Crosby caught sight of us approaching and glared over my left shoulder, as a police officer held Crosby's head and pushed him down into the back seat of the squad car. The two officers that arrested him were not the ones who brought Drake to me. The first police car had taken Burne directly to jail from the hilltop.

Shelta had her arms around Ryker, who was on her lap cuddling her. Uny was next to them on the couch in Shelta's apartment. Uny jumped up to hug me. We shook as uncontrollable tears flowed freely from both of us.

Drake softly inquired, "Shelta, you okay?"

She looked down at the top of Ryker's head and looked up again to barely shake her head no. "I need to get Ryker to bed."

"Hey, buddy. Would you let me help you get ready for bed tonight?"

Ryker looked at his mamai for approval. He slid off the couch to take Drake's extended hand, and they went upstairs to his room. As the bedroom door was closing, I heard Drake ask, "Which drawer holds the jammies?"

Ryker replied, "The police took my pa."

I mopped up my face with a couple of tissues from the box on Shelta's end table and sat down next to Shelta. I put my arm around her. She leaned her head onto my shoulder.

"You warned me, Grace. I was in denial. In spite of his foul temper, there was no way I thought he could have murdered anyone. In so many ways, it seemed like underneath all that confusing bluster, he was a kind man."

"Yes, he was. Bitterness is a cruel master that destroys people. Even kind people. He had so much hatred toward our pa and Paddy over the Doohickey. His greed for their residual payments must have been eating at him too, yet he was going to use some of his blood money to be kind. Remember the way he immediately offered to pay for Uny's care and delivery?"

"Grace, I don't know if I have enough to keep his promise. He was probably counting on money coming in from somewhere because our bank accounts are not all that plush right now."

I told her my guess. "He was counting on a huge chunk of life insurance. He was going to kill my pa. I overheard him on the phone planning it to be an accident, but not like Collen's. After he left the office, I found a receipt for a truck that matches the description of the one that killed Collen. He rented it, but never returned it. Paid the replacement price instead. But he forgot his gym ID, so he came back and caught me. That's why he had Burne take me to a cliff to kill me."

She sat up straight and tense. "What? Are you kidding? Is that where you've been?"

"Yes. Drake saw us leave here, called the police, got Uny's phone from her," I smiled at my sister, "and followed us using GPS."

"Thank God for Drake and GPS! You'd be dead!"

"Well, maybe not dead, but definitely thank God. Burne changed his mind."

Drake came out of Ryker's room and relaxed into Crosby's easy chair. Uny sat down on the other side of Shelta and tucked her arm around us behind Shelta's waist.

For Drake's sake, I repeated how it all went down, how I'd heard Crosby talking about an accident for pa like Collen, how I'd started snooping, and how Crosby came back for his gym badge and caught me right after I had faxed the invoice to Zane.

"He didn't realize you'd already faxed it?"

"He thought I had tried to make a copy, not send a fax. While he was taping me to the chair, he mumbled something about no paper in the copier."

Shelta rolled her eyes. "That's not surprising; I don't think he understands most of the office devices."

I smiled. "I believe you. You should have seen him with the packing tape dispenser." I continued with all the details of how Burne had been so kind to me, about our trip to the cliff, and how Burne had decided to kill himself instead of me.

While I was telling my story, Uny looked suddenly distressed. She left us momentarily and, listening from the kitchen, came back with a tall glass of ice water with a straw. She handed to me with her eyes brimming again. "Oh, Grace." She sat down again next to Shelta.

I gratefully drank some water.

Drake declared, "I think we should call you Amazing Grace."

I felt my cheeks grow warm. "Well I don't know if I'd go that far, but it's probably time for me to quit the name Gypsy Grace."

"Oh, me too!" Uny turned to face Shelta. "It's okay about Crosby's promise. No more gypsy life for me. I want to go home."

CHAPTER THIRTY-SIX

Email to Josie

Grace to Josie:

I'm reading your last email. You said it couldn't get any worse. Would this be worse? I overheard Crosby on the phone saying he was planning to kill my pa and make it look like an accident, but not the same accident they caused for my fiancé, Collen. He had been talking to Burne.

Crosby bound and gagged me.

Burne took me to a ridgetop to murder me.

A miracle happened: Burne changed his mind and let me go. He intended to dive off the ridgetop to his death, but I talked him out of it. Drake brought the police to the ridgetop using Uny's phone to track mine with GPS. They arrived before Burne had a chance to change his mind again.

Crosby and Burne are both in jail. Burne is going to testify against his father.

So, other than being kidnapped and the fact that I'm going to take Uny home (by airplane!) not much happening here. LOL.

And you're right. I'm not going to go home in defeat. I'm going to stand up for what's right for myself and both of my sisters. With this resolve, I may not be welcome, but I'll face whatever is waiting there for me. I'm determined to make a difference in the world. I'm going to start at home.

But enough about me. How are things with you?

CHAPTER THIRTY-SEVEN

Goodbyes

We planned to leave Pacific Grove at the end of the week. I had enough saved to book us on a one-way flight from Monterey to Austin. Since it seemed so inexpensive, I wondered how it compared to the price of a bus trip, especially compared to the cost of ours.

Standing on the deck by the shore, I pondered our upcoming adjustment to Texas heat. I'd become accustomed to cool breezes, the sound of crashing waves all hours of the day and night, barking seals, and noisy seabirds. My heart ached each time I thought about saying good-bye to Shelta, Ryker, and Drake. However, I got a little thrill throughout my body with each thought of Zane. It would be so great to see him again. He and I had chatted several times each day, either by text or in short, live conversations. He sent me images of flowers after each. I asked him how long ago he had upgraded to a smartphone. When he told me the timing, I said, "I wish I had known that." I'll never know if it would have made any difference if I hadn't had to wait for the fax machine. It may have meant that Crosby would have caught me with my phone in my hand and taken it away.

I felt Uny arrive at my side. "I'm sure going to miss this."

"Hi Uny. I was just thinking that."

She asked, "Have you also been thinking about facing Pa, as I have?"

I turned to her and smiled. "You sure know how to kill a mood."

"I know, right? I'm the voice of doom to your lovely ocean afternoon. What do you think? Will he go ballistic?"

"I don't know. He might, but I called him this morning, and he didn't yell at me."

"You did? You are so brave. I've never known anyone as brave as you are."

"I gave him our flight number and arrival time. He assured me he'd pick us up at the airport and that probably Mamai would be there too. She came home from the hospital yesterday."

Uny's eyes filled with tears. "Oh, Mamai!"

I took her in my arms. "I know. I can't wait to see her either." I released Uny from our hug. "Well, I don't expect that Pa will show his temper at the airport."

"No, I'm sure he'll wait until he gets us home. And then, if he's trying to be nice, I can ruin it all and tell him I'm pregnant."

"Now look who's brave."

"Yeah, well I've had a lot of time to think about this and I've decided, I *am* brave. In one of those novels that Drake brought me, there's a single mom who was forsaken as I sort of have been. The protagonist in that novel chose bravely to raise her child alone. Her determination to do what was right and good was an inspiration to me."

"You didn't really give your rapist the choice to forsake you though, remember?"

"Yeah, well, there's that. I'm exercising my 'right to choose' in a unique way. I was nothing to the guy who did this to me, other than a piece of trash to use and discard—

you know what? I'm not going to go there. We didn't know each other. However, you are correct. I'm not giving him a choice."

"You are actually freeing him to make future choices. We know he drugged you and he seduced you. Your decision not to prosecute him is keeping him from possible incarceration. You may be keeping him free to harm someone else. Have you thought of that?"

"No. I probably should. I promise I will consider taking action against him but not right now. My baby's well-being comes first. I'm working on staying at peace, trying not to blame or generate negative thoughts of vengeance or even remorse." She patted her tummy. "This is a gift, no matter how unintended. I can probably take action against him without telling him he fathered a child. One thing at a time. I could do that someday, stand up to prevent him from hurting others but not with a pregnant belly and all pregnancy-associated emotions. I'm willing to face the embarrassment someday, but today is not that day."

"So for your body and the baby's sake, you're taking the position, 'Whatever is true, whatever is noble, whatever is right, whatever is pure, whatever is lovely, whatever is admirable—if anything is excellent or praiseworthy—think about such things?'"

"Exactly. Don't you love having your own Bible? Who knew it could be such an encouragement?"

"Right? I think pretty much everyone besides us has known it for a long time. Then there are probably many who are afraid if they read it, they might have to be accountable. I bet they would be pleasantly surprised how God and His Bible are tremendously encouraging."

"And surprised at how often He tells us within it how much He loves us."

"Oh, Uny. I'm so proud of you. Everyone makes mistakes, but our failures are not what define us; it is how we respond to them that characterizes who we are. You are a wonderful, godly woman."

Uny lifted one eyebrow. "We'll see how wonderful, godly, and brave I am when I actually face Pa."

On our last night in Pacific Grove, Shelta invited Drake to dinner. I fixed a slow-roasted garlic pork roast. Instead of potatoes, I made some brown rice, refried beans, salsa, and homemade tortilla chips, plus a crispy green salad.

Shelta exclaimed, "I can't believe you waited until now to prepare roast pork! You've got to teach me how to make this."

Drake's mood was subdued. "It won't be the same around here without you. Right, Ryker?"

"Yeah, first my pa leaves. Now you."

"Oh gosh, Ryker. I'm so sad we are leaving you too. We both are, right Uny?"

Uny nodded. She looked too emotional to speak.

"Yes, sweetheart. We will miss you too. But guess what? We just found out how much it costs to fly from where we live to here and it's not that much. We'll come to visit you. In the meantime, we can Facetime on your mom's phone or Skype on her computer."

"Really?"

"Yes. Shelta, I know you don't allow us to use phones at the dinner table, but may I do a demonstration for Ryker?"

Shelta put a forkful of pork on top of one of the chips. "Go ahead, but you're missing out on the best dinner I've ever tasted in my life."

"So glad you're enjoying it." I slipped my phone out of my pocket, chose Shelta, and tapped Facetime.

When her phone rang in her pocket, she took it out and handed it to Ryker. "Tap that button."

Ryker started giggling when he saw my picture on the phone's screen. He could also hear his giggling from my phone across the table. He exclaimed, "This is so cool!" As did the echo from my phone.

"And this," I echoed to the still giggling Ryker, "is how we will talk face to face when we are miles from each other, my dear cousin."

I captured a screenshot of his grinning face before we hung up from our demonstration to enjoy the pork.

"There is a distinct possibility, I won't be welcome at home when I tell my pa my terms."

Shelta's eyes watered up, "You will always be welcome here. And I got some good news today. I'll probably be able to be right here when you come back. I was afraid that the insurance company would want the money back for Collen's insurance if Crosby gets convicted of murdering him, but no. I was the second beneficiary, and they fully intend to honor the payout."

"Shelta. That's so good. I'm happy for you and Ryker."

In spite of great food, good news, and technological entertainment, it was a sad evening. Uny and I loved these people, and our heart ached for Shelta who would be on her own, regardless of the outcome of Crosby's trial in Texas. He could get life in prison or the death penalty. Many of the states who still have the death penalty haven't executed any inmates for five years. Texas is not one of them.

As much as I would miss Shelta and Ryker though, when I was saying goodbye to Drake I felt like Dorothy in the Wizard of Oz when she told the scarecrow, "I'll miss you most of all."

Drake made certain something was extremely clear, "I don't do Facetime, Grace."

We were taking an after-dinner walk along the tumbling, whispering green silver of the water. Seaspray hit a rock, and the ever-present breezes brought them near us on the shore. Halfa moon was in the west surrounded by a bazillion stars. The only mist was in my eyes.

"Why not?"

"Because every time I accidentally turn the camera on myself, I think, *who's that old man with the weathered face?*"

"Oh, Drake you're so silly."

"You just wait. When that youthful face with the flawless skin starts to falter, you'll be calling Ryker the old fashion way."

"You're a good friend, Drake." I felt my throat tighten and gulped it away.

"It's been an honor to be your friend, Gypsy, I mean, Amazing Grace."

"I am grateful for you and your support for both Uny and me. I'm also grateful you are a friend to Cousin Shelta and Ryker. Especially now when they need you."

"Yes. Shelta and I moved from an employer/employee relationship to friends a long time ago." He stopped at one of the coves we knew so well to watch the unique swell and swirl that foamed the waves into circles that seemed to dance with each other. "She and I have talked a few times since Crosby's arrest. I'll be here to help her in every way I can, including with Ryker." He paused to stare at waves swirling their do-si-do. "Poor Ryker. He was really fond of Burne."

"I know. On the way to what was supposed to be my execution, I told Burne that I didn't suppose a murderer stops to think how taking the life of one person affects the lives of so many others. Those thoughts were about how Burne's actions affected so many of the lives connected with Collen." I sighed. "And now, there are the lives connected to Burne." I paused to think about what I had said. "Burne loves Ryker. Maybe if he doesn't get the death penalty, he'll have a chance to reach out to Ryker."

"Wow, you really are Amazing Grace. You didn't only convince him not to Peter Pan off that ridge, you talked him out of murdering you, didn't you?"

"I don't know. There was a lot of kindness toward me long before I convinced him that he needed to testify to put a stop to his pa's murderous greed. I'd like to think he had enough conscience within his own soul to make the right decisions that night."

"If Burne reached out to him, do you think it would be good for Ryker?"

"I do. When I talked Burne out of going off that cliff, he didn't change his mind because of me. He changed it because he was contrite before God. I'm convinced that God is not done with Burne. He's never done with anyone, no matter how harshly the rest of us are judging that person. God is a rewarder of those who earnestly seek Him. I'm afraid a lot of people don't understand what it means when God says 'all' or 'the world' or 'whosoever.' Burne might be the only one who can help Ryker get over what Crosby has done."

He stood there grinning at me.

"What?"

"Oh, nothing, Amazing Grace. So what now? You're going back to the cult. Are you going to follow your father's wishes to marry Zane's father?"

"Now you're just picking on me. You know the answer to that."

"Yeah. I do. Let's head back." He put his brotherly arm around my shoulders and turned me toward the home I'd known for the past six months. My home for one more night.

I said to him, "I suppose I didn't need to run away. I merely needed to stand up for what is right."

CHAPTER THIRTY-EIGHT

Homecoming

In only six months, Mamai's auburn hair had been quietly taken over by strands of pure white, but she was smiling and she seemed to have her wits about her. I hoped that the visible, loving emotion on her face meant her happiness was not merely drug induced. She raised a feathery eyebrow and smiled as we approached her. It was a bit intriguing, as if she held a secret. I looked at Pa and thought to myself, *Here is where the secret lies.* He looked different. This man, who had always been in control, who never showed emotion, or as far as I could tell, never felt emotions, looked contrite. His eyes were wet.

Uny and I took turns hugging everyone though grateful tears.

Mamai was crying, "My daughter, my daughter."

Pa smiled. "Welcome home, girls."

I spoke for both of us. "Thank you for having us back."

I mumbled to each of them how much I loved them and missed them and added, "Billy." You have grown.

"Danee, you look so beautiful"

I was grateful for the welcome, and it was good to hear Pa say it was still our home, but we still had Uny's news to share. I had pondered this on the plane. We had no idea what Mamai had told Pa, if anything, or how well she could play her part if she was still play-acting ignorance. Historically, it took little to rouse his anger. Revealing that she already knew about Uny's condition or that she had been in touch with us might set him off like fireworks. Unless I could snatch a few moments with Mamai alone, my plan was to approach Pa with whatever lies required to protect Mamai. In my rebellion and escape to California and in all that had happened to Uny and me there, I'd learned a little about the secret Zane was trying to share with me. Some things that ring true need to be experienced before we understand what we know, like the mystery and victory of faith. It was not enough to understand that I needed to surrender to overcome my guilt and so many other indications that I was not dead to myself, like my judgmental attitude. I needed to actually surrender. Yet here, at this juncture, mere willingness didn't seem to be sufficient. In my upcoming interview with Pa, the reality was, I didn't trust God enough to honor Him with total integrity. In my heart, I wanted to start fresh with Pa, in an honest relationship, but it was too risky. I feared Pa's anger would flare up and destroy Mamai's fragile mental balance. He need never know her part in our escape from his tyranny. My conversation was fraught with possible failure, one way or another. All I could do was pray, "I apologize in advance for my conditional surrender. I believe You will be with us in that room; help my unbelief that may keep me from trusting You."

His gray eyes were as flat and unreadable as chips of flint. We were in his den with the door closed. Pa was in his office chair. I'd never noticed previously how his chair strategically placed him in a dominating position a few inches above the person the opposing guest chair, who at this moment was me. I sat as tall as I could and returned his intent stare. My nerves had climbed up into my shoulders and neck. "You don't have to explain how you left without a trace."

"I'm not sure I could anyway."

"Where have you been? Near Monterey, I take it."

"Yes. We've been staying with Crosby and his wife, Mamai's Cousin Shelta."

The blood turned his face bright red. "That murderer! You heard he's been arrested for killing Collen? He and that son of his, Burne."

I lifted my cup of tea to my mouth in a vain attempt to swallow down the lump in my throat. I set it carefully into its saucer. "Yes. I'm the one who found evidence. I faxed it to Zane." Now was not the time to tell the rest of the story entirely. It would have to wait until family anxieties and tensions calmed. *Perhaps I'll write about it someday.*

His bushy eyebrows crushed together with sharp vertical lines between them, then he nodded his head as if he was beginning to understand, "Zane. The boy didn't tell me that he got that from you."

"He's not a boy."

"Too true, too true. No insult intended. You'll see when you get old though. Everyone in the next generation stays as if they are children to you, even when they're far past childhood."

"You were next on Crosby's hit list."

The former redness paled away from his face entirely. "Seriously?"

"Yes, but they moved me up in the murder queue when they caught me with that evidence."

"So it seems you have saved my life. And they tried to kill *you*?"

"That's a long story. They intended to kill me. They kidnapped me, but Burne had a change of heart."

Again, his expressive eyebrows turned his face into a question mark.

"May I tell that story later, please? We have more important things to talk about."

"Your mamai fell apart after you left."

"I'm so sorry. I know. I talked to Zane."

"So you stayed in touch with him the whole time you were gone?"

"No. Zane was not part of the beginning of the story, the part from which you released me, remember?" I smiled.

He smiled back at me. "I've underestimated you your whole life, haven't I?"

"Probably.

"Let me say this, Zane was not involved with our leaving in any way. I got in touch with him later, okay?"

There was great restraint evident in the tightness of his jaw. I saw a vein beating in his temple, up near the hairline. This was not easy for him. In my heart, I commended him for trying.

"Go on, Daughter. What is it that's got you so worked up that we needed to come here and talk it out alone?"

"There are two important things, Pa. I'll take the easiest one first. You probably suspect what it is."

He looked at me carefully, almost solemnly, as if he were trying to read my features like a book in a foreign language. "Could you have known I was betrothing you to Paddy?"

"Good guess. Uny and I overheard you. I didn't leave just because I didn't want to marry Paddy. I could not live in the same house with Zane as his pa's wife."

"You're sweet on Zane." He nodded as if he knew it all along, then his expression turned dark, "But you took Uny too."

"Yes, sir. She and I figured if I left, you might betroth her to Paddy in my place, and although on her part there's no romantic interest in Zane, she was totally grossed out at the thought of marrying someone as old as you." I turned my palms up. It was sort of a relegation, "over to you."

"All the Travelers' ways are engrained in me and all of my own ways as well." He sat silent for a moment, as if letting his own words sink in. "Haven't really considered others in my decisions because, I suppose I knew in part that I could get away with it. I was in control and expected everyone to obey. I thought you all looked up to me for it."

"If you equate fearing you with looking up to you."

"I was mad when you left." His face got red again, but I sensed embarrassment, not anger. "I threw out all your stuff or gave it to St. Vincent de Paul. During that fit of anger, I was thinking I'd get rid of it so you could never come back for it, and that I'd never welcome you back at all. I was frustrated with your mamai. Resented that she could go crazy and leave me to take care of everything by myself."

"What changed?"

When she had her first breakdown, did you know she had two? She had a second one that put her in the hospital for a while, in fact, she just got out the other day. Zane told you, right?"

"Yes." I felt tears sting suddenly behind my eyes.

He saw my emotion and seemed moved with kindness I hadn't expected. "Your mamai's psychiatrist, Olivia, the one I sent your mamai to after her first breakdown, thought it would help Anita if I would come for a few sessions without your mamai, only me."

I smiled. "Just a few?"

"You're a sharp one, aren't you Grace?"

"I come from the sharpest. Were you so sharp that you had an epiphany in three sessions?"

"She asked me hard questions like, 'Do you think you will ever be able to forgive them?' and 'Do you want your daughters to be miserable the rest of their lives because they defied you and ran away?'"

"And?"

"I'm still seeing her twice a week."

"Good for you Pa. Really good. It's not easy to humble yourself and be willing to make changes. I'm proud of you. You may not believe this, but everyone will look up to you more for being a benevolent, forgiving head of the family, instead of one who causes us to tremble in fear."

"But you came back." His large finger pointed to himself, then to me, and back toward himself again. He shook his head. "So you don't fear me anymore?"

"I certainly wouldn't say that." I scoffed. "We came back in spite of our fear. As bold and courageous as it looks to you— me sitting across from you here in your den—doesn't mean I'm not afraid." I offered a gentle smile. "And I won't be staying if you still insist on continuing in the ways of the cult."

"Cult!" He shouted at me.

Tension climbed along my spine. I stared at him for two eternal minutes with my commonsense in fragments and my imagination racing madly through a series of nightmare pictures of anger and violence directed toward me, toward Uny. I answered as calmly as possible, "Yes, cult." I defiantly slipped my phone from my pocket and tapped it several times, and read out loud, "A relatively small group of people having religious beliefs or practices regarded by others as strange or sinister."

I saw blind rage give way to some kind of reason. It was like watching a stone mask come alive. "I suppose it is."

"Kudos to you Pa. Please keep going to Olivia." I paused to take a calming breath. "Does that mean Uny and I are still welcome here?"

"Yes, Daughter, please stay and we'll figure out a new way. It won't be easy for me to change. We may have a bumpy path for a while and need a few more meetings like this."

"I know." I took a slow, deep breath. "And now the hard part."

"Harder than what you went through, what you put your mother and me through, and harder than you and Uny breaking away from everything we've known all your lives?"

"Yes." Uny's pregnant."

The knuckles of his hands turned white against the edge of his desk. The vein on his forehead began to pulse again. His jaw tightened as if he was clenching his teeth. "This is your fault!"

I stayed tall in my chair. "Is it?"

He leaned forward; his face and neck got redder than I had ever seen it. "Don't you think it's your fault?"

"I did at first. Blamed myself entirely, but can you understand why I don't now?"

He released his grip on his desk and sat back. "You blame me, don't you?"

"No. I don't blame you or myself or even Uny. I don't blame you because you didn't drive her to make the choices she made, but neither do I think you could have prevented her from going a little wild had she stayed here. I think she would have eventually sought to be free and was as prone to naiveté in Texas as she was in California. And blame doesn't change the past, but forgiveness does. Since God forgives us, instead of blaming everyone or anyone, can't we forgive each other and forgive ourselves?"

The redness faded from his face. "Forgiveness." Whatever pain he was feeling caused his eyes to brim with tears. He bowed his head and softly muttered, "No." Then he nodded. "Yes." His den was not prepared for this. There were no tissues in sight.

Not fully trusting to make it through this interview without needing a tissue myself, I had come prepared. I pulled a one from my jean's pocket, came around the desk, and handed it to him. Then I hugged his shoulders. "Oh, Pa. I know. I know." He hugged me back with one arm. I almost cried too, but I gained strength from somewhere to maintain my composure. I returned to the guest chair and gave him time. I sat watching the shadows of the branches outside the window dancing in the gleaming wood of Pa's desk.

At last, he spoke. "You seem to have everything figured out. Now what?"

I told him then about the date rape and how Uny chose not to prosecute her rapist and refused to involve the scoundrel in any way or to even let him know she was pregnant. I told him that she might seek prosecution someday. There were results of tests that would prove he drugged her, but for now, she felt the appropriate punishment for him was to prevent him from having any rights to their child. I assured Pa that Uny and the baby were in good health and told him how Crosby paid for early prenatal visits and vitamins, how he had promised to pay for the delivery as well.

He looked astounded. "Isn't that strange? So much hatred toward me all those years, even planning to bump me off for insurance, and yet he helped my daughter."

"I know, right? Shelta and I wondered if it may have been an extension of his spite by hiding the news from you because Uny wouldn't need to use your health insurance. But who knows? I guess people who do bad things are not necessarily entirely bad."

He shot a look directly into my eyes, "And some seemingly sweet people have a mean streak."

"Yes. I suppose that's true too. I understand how deeply I hurt you. I didn't want to, but I knew it would. You may not believe this, but I didn't do it out of meanness. Can you understand how I felt I had no choice?"

We sat in the silence of bad memories.

Pa's fight with emotion was far from over. He angrily patted his face beneath one eye then looked down at his untouched teacup before pouring the entire, cooled contents down his throat. He wiped his mouth with his hand. "Didn't Uny want to come home to have her baby?"

"From the first, she wanted to give her baby up for adoption. She is convinced it's a girl, though no one has confirmed that yet." I grinned.

"And the way things were when you left, she would never bring a girl to be raised here, right?"

"Yes. She said that. But she also said she wanted her baby to have two parents who loved her, and she didn't want her daughter to someday challenge or question Uny about how it happened or somesuch. Things could change, but she still felt the same when we talked during the plane ride home from California. I think Uny may reconsider when she settles back into Mamai's loving care and sees your change of heart and rules. We'll see. I'm proud of her though. She didn't go all drama queen or get rebellious and continue on her path of self-destruction. She bucked up and accepted responsibility for her actions and her future. She has grown up, especially spiritually."

He nodded in agreement; my pa, the former despot king, agreed, "I'm proud of her too."

CHAPTER THIRTY-NINE

Zane Reunion

Mamai looked radiant and mysterious as she set the dining room table. "No, Grace, I don't need any help. I'll ask Danee to help serve at the very end, but I want the kitchen to myself as I prepare this meal. Go. Primp. You look beautiful, but go make yourself even more so before Zane gets here."

"Okay, if you're sure." I headed upstairs but looked back over my shoulder, "I still can't believe Pa invited him." Danee was in my room. "Hi!" I gave her a hug.

"What was that for?"

"Because I can."

"Oh, Grace. I've really missed you. I'm so glad you guys are back. I have a surprise for you."

I hadn't noticed it before. She picked my jewelry box up from the top of my bed and handed it to me.

"Oh, Danee! I thought Pa gave it all away."

"He did, but while he was throwing everything into garbage bags, I asked him if he would give me this."

I set the box onto its spot on the empty dresser and looked sadly at the empty display shelf above it where my dolls formerly sat in their pretty dresses. I opened the jewelry box and pulled out my birthstone necklace. "Will you work the clasp for me, please? Zane's coming to dinner. I'd like to wear it." I got it into position and turned my back to her, handing her both sides of the clasp.

She hooked it. "I have your dolls too."

I turned and embraced her again. "You're the best!"

"I had Uny's dolls and jewelry too. I already gave them to her while you were in lockdown with Pa." She headed out the door saying, "I'll get your dolls."

When Zane arrived, Mamai told us dinner was not quite ready and suggested we go for a walk.

"Shall we sit there?" Zane pointed to the picnic table where we had first rendezvoused after running together. Where Mamai, Uny, and I plotted our escape. I learned later that it was the same table where Mamai had her second breakdown. It was where she handed Zane her phone.

"Listen." Hundreds of birds were chirping above us in the canopy of trees. "Time was, time is, and time will be, and yet the birds still sit in the trees and sing."

Zane grinned at me. "Sounds like poem fodder. You've been through a lot since we sat here listening to noisy birds."

"I have, but what's more important than what I've been through, is how I learned the things you were trying to teach me about living victoriously. And, while I was learning, I bonded with people along the way."

"You made some friends?"

"Yes. Good friends. Uny and I met someone named Josie on our bus trip. She lives in Phoenix. We email. I also fell in love with someone named Ryker." I gave him a sly smile.

Zane lifted his eyebrows. "Serious competition?"

I could tell I hadn't shaken his confidence. "No. He turned seven just before I left California. I also truly love my cousin and friend, Shelta. Ryker is her son. I promised to visit them regularly. Of course, I'll have to put up with the cool ocean breezes, the pounding waves against the shore, the barking seals, and the noise from a bazillion sea birds."

"Sounds like you could suffer through that to visit your friends."

"And Drake."

"More competition?"

"No. A great friend, kind of like a big brother. You'll like him."

"You're inviting me to go to California with you?"

"Probably." We listened to the birds for a few minutes. "It's good to be back. It seems this was as good a place as any to make a difference, and it's my home. I kept thinking I had to help the world in big, massive, multiple ways, but when it comes down to it, it's really only one person at a time, like Josie, or Burne."

"Who's Burne?"

"I'll tell you at dinner. I have a story to tell everyone. What is it Zane? You look guilty."

"Nope, I told you I know how to get past my guilt."

"Then you must be up to something."

Mamai made the same meatloaf she made the night before we left. Pa looked around the table suspiciously but apparently decided not to cause a disturbance. I considered his promise to me that he would not ask me for details of our middle-of-the-night escape from home, and I presumed that he may not want to know if Mamai was part of it. I also pondered how God had honored my prayer of conditional surrender. He allowed me to honor Him with integrity, without compromising Mamai's secret scheme. In deep gratitude, I struggled against ensuing tears.

I savored a slice of Mamai's warm homemade bread with melting butter before I related the whole story about being caught by Crosby and kidnapped by Burne. For Zane's sake, I left out the part about Burne kissing me on the cheek when he changed his mind about killing me or himself.

Uny got into the story to make sure everyone knew she gave her phone to Drake, and it was her phone's GPS that saved me.

Danee asked, "Who is Drake?"

I let Uny describe our baby seal tour guide, the motel handyman, and friend who rescued Uny the worst night of her life. She told us how Drake had an ex-wife, Paige, and a daughter, Lily, and that he was friends with his ex. She told us how the wholesome books Paige had loaned her contained stories that helped Uny climb out of her confusion, not just temporarily. Next, she launched into the complete tale of Loosey on the loose. And how her concern for Loosey was also an inspiration for her recent decision.

Zane asked, "Really? How so?"

Mamai grinned. "Zane, we're going to have another member of the family living here."

"Yes. I'm going to have a baby." Uny turned to me, "And, I'm going to keep her."

Danee, clapped her hands together, "A baby!"

I looked at Mamai and Pa and knew they had already been touched by this grandchild. This baby would change everyone's life for the better. Mamai would have a reason to do the work to keep her sanity. As Johan's death broke her, love for, and from, her grandchild would help heal the brokenness. Pa would keep toiling toward the changes in himself to strengthen his wife's mental health and create new bonds of love and loyalty in his family. This tiny person would bring love and purpose for both of them and for all of us. I thought, *This then must be why Mamai had been so giddy all day.*

Billy asked, "A baby? Wow! If it's a boy, he can share my room."

Zane announced, "There will be a spare room."

A thrill of excitement surged throughout my brain and body as I watched him push back his chair and get down on one knee next to mine. A ring box materialized from somewhere. "I have permission from your pa," he emphasized the next three words, "and your mamai." He bowed slightly to my reformed, kingly pa. "Grace, will you marry me?"

THANK YOU AND ABOUT THE AUTHOR

Thank you for reading Gypsy Grace. I would be most grateful if you would post a brief, honest review on Amazon.com. Thank you in advance,

Joan Bannan, author, storyteller, prayer warrior.

"Great stories don't require profanity"

It can be difficult, but it is a priority for me as a storyteller to write without content and language that I would regret hearing if it replayed in my mind.

Many of us, who prefer not to hear profanity, are surrounded by it. Some of us love to read, but hesitate to escape into the stress-relieving, lifelong enjoyment of novels because we may be subject to word pictures painted onto our inner screen that we will be unable to unsee.

My goal as an author is to listen to the still, small voice that inspires me to write with savory salt for the soul as I sing to myself, "This little light of mine, I'm gonna let it shine."

I am a student of Ted Dekker's Creative Way Course in Transformational Fiction and numerous other storytelling and novel-writing tomes. I'm the author of four non-fiction books and now four novels. I love birds and flowers, especially roses. My millennial son, Peter, my parakeet, and two box turtles keep me company in my home in a small city in Northern California.

I love to hear from my readers. Please visit my Just Joan Bannan Facebook page at https://www.facebook.com/justjoanbannan or my website at http://bannan.com where you can sign up for my not-so-frequent e-newsletters.

Other novels by Joan Bannan

Halfa Moon

Twintuition

The Treasure of Granzella Ranch

DISCUSSION QUESTIONS

1. When Grace feels guilty for not grieving for Collen, do you think her guilt was well-founded?

2. If you were Shelta, would you have married Crosby?

3. Drake says he was married once and he knew that it would be only once for him. To you think anyone can actually stick to that resolve in this day and age?

4. Do you think Grace should have stayed true to Zane and not accepted a date with Burne?

5. Why do you think Crosby offered to pay for Uny's health care?

6. Do you think Burne really cared about Grace and was possibly falling in love with her, or do you think what was going on was all about him and an extension of who he was?

7. If you were in Uny's situation, would you have pursued prosecution of the rapist?

RECIPES

Marylyn's Meatloaf

This unique recipe is from my Cousin Marylyn Caliendo. Neither she nor I measure, but if you are willing to try this with my "about this much" or "As-much-as-you-think-you'd-like" instructions you will not be disappointed.

About a pound of ground beef

A cup or so cooked rice (I use brown rice. Marylyn uses Japanese sticky white rice.)

About a tablespoon of Soy Sauce

About a quarter of a cup dried minced onion

Two eggs

About a quarter of cup of milk

Garlic powder

Parsley

Chopped celery

Pepper

Chaka's MMM sauce on top. If you can't find Chaka's, its first ingredient is soy sauce so you could probably substitute with that.

350 for about an hour

Buttery Potatoes

Amounts: Lots of butter per potato, like a half a cube per two large potatoes, a whole cube for several potatoes.

Peel potatoes and cut them into French fry shapes. I prefer firmer potatoes like fingerling, golden, or red, but any potato is fine.

Heat a heavy bottom pan.

Melt the butter, add the potatoes, and cover. Maintain medium flame.

Turn frequently. They will get crispy brown.

Remove from pan. Sprinkle immediately with coarse salt and dried dill.

The firmer potatoes can usually be picked up with your fingers. You'll need a fork for softer ones.

Pork Roast - Shoulder roast, sometimes called "butt"

I often cut the roast into pieces that will fit into a pan that I want to use. Choose a pan that has a lid. I've used Country spare ribs when they are on sale.

Coarsely chop about 12 – 20 cloves of garlic, depending on the size of your roast.

Sprinkle liberally with garlic salt and pepper. Put it fat side up into a roasting pan or Dutch oven that has a good lid.

Sprinkle with some soy sauce, the juice of a lemon or two and some olive oil. Spread the chopped garlic all over both sides. If you like spice, sprinkle on some red pepper flakes.

Put about a half of a cup of chicken broth in the bottom.

Cover with the lid.

Bake at around 275 for about 5 hours or so, till the meat pulls apart easily with a fork.

You can cook a huge roast overnight, more like 8 to 12 hours depending on the size.

It's great on sandwiches or in a salad.

My favorite way to eat it leftover:

Make a slaw from sliced cabbage, chopped green onions, chopped jalapeños, salt and lime juice.

Soften a tortilla in olive oil, plop in some warmed up pork and top with cabbage slaw.

It's also great in Burritos or Chimichangas.

Extraordinary Chicken Salad

This was originally a Tuna Salad recipe that said, "Or cooked chicken."

Cooked chicken breast

1 can water chestnuts chopped

1 cup chopped celery

1 can sliced black olives

1 small bell pepper, diced

1/2 cup chopped green onions

Dressing:

1 cup mayonnaise

1 T wine vinegar

1 t or so garlic salt

Mix everything together, add dressing and chill. If I'm going to have it on hand for lunches, I often leave the green onions until the last minute and add them with one of the following just before serving:

1 can little French fries.

Canned Chinese noodles.

Cashews.

Peanuts.

Or my favorite: Buttery Toasted Slivered Almonds:

Warm a heavy bottom pan. Add a couple tablespoons of butter, then several Tablespoons of raw slivered almonds. Toss around frequently on low heat, being diligent to remove from heat as soon as they start to brown. Add a pinch of coarse salt. I sometimes toss in some sesame seed as the slivers are toasting. Store in the refrigerator to add crunch to any salad.

Peters Ground Beef, Broccoli, Cauliflower and Tots Casserole

1 to 1.5 pounds ground beef

1 medium onion

2 -3 cloves minced garlic

Garlic salt, pepper, and olive oil

1 head of broccoli (7 – 10 flowerets)

7 – 10 flowerets of cauliflower.

About 3 cups White Sauce (or cream of mushroom soup)

Tots

Sharp Cheddar cheese slices (or grated would work too).

Optional: mix Cheddar with Monterey Jack.

Brown meat with chopped onions in olive oil, adding garlic salt and pepper (I like a lot of pepper with beef).

Cut the broccoli and cauliflower into bite-size heads.

Put the cauliflower on top of the cooked meat. Cover to steam the cauliflower for several minutes before adding the broccoli.

Give the pan a stir. Put the broccoli on top of the cooked meat and cover again. Cook until the broccoli is bright green.

Pour into a casserole dish, add white sauce, and mix well.

Cover completely with tots and bake at 375 or 400 (or convection) for about 25 – 30 minutes.

Remove from oven.

Cover tots with cheese, put back into oven for another 5 or 10 minutes, just until the cheese melts.

ACKNOWLEDGMENTS

I'm most grateful for ...

Content Editing, Brainstorming, and Ideas:
Tina Fikejs

Sandy Isganitis

Copy editors:
Susan Batty

Tina Fikejs

Sandy Isganitis

Audiobook narrator:
Tina Marie Fikejs

Advice and support:
Fred Rich New York Life Insurance

Formatting and cover:
Gypsy Grace Portrait: Sherre Bernardo

eBook launch

P and G Graphics

Photography:
Bryan Batty

Best Meatloaf recipe ever:

Marylyn Caliendo

Writing resources:

Ted Dekker's Creative Way Writing Course

Invisible Ink:

A PRACTIAL GUID TO BUIDLING STORIES THAT RESONATE

Brian McDonald

2017 ISBN 978-0-9985344-7-3

45 Master Characters

Mythic Models for Creating Original Characters

Victoria Lynn Schmidt

2001 ISBN 1-58297-069-6